NOW AND THEN

Jonathan D. Scott

MIDDLETON BOOKS

www.middletonbooks.com

First edition 2026. Printed in the USA.

Cover and book design: Jonathan D. Scott
Cover painting "Westtown Lake" (1975)

Library of Congress Control Number: 2025948502

Foreword

I remember writing short stories as a child on a manual typewriter that belonged to my father. I returned to writing in the early 1980s, at that time on an electric typewriter which was my own. I had some initial success, but stopped writing short stories to attend to my life's demands until the beginning of the twenty-first century—after I had written and published *Lenegrin* and the *Woman in the Wilderness*. By that time, I owned a computer, and it was possible to submit stories to both online and print literary journal electronically—far easier than going to a copy shop, slipping pages into a large envelope, buying postage, and biding my time until I heard back by post.

I took another break from short stories until after I moved to Lexington, KY in 2022. The tastes in fiction of literary journals had largely outgrown my own inclinations. Still, a few editors accepted some of what I submitted.

The foregoing is the reason for the title of this collection. These stories span over 40 years, and my writing has always been just now and then.

I don't know what kind of reader you might be with an interest in this collection. Whoever you are, I ask that you give some understanding for my being a product of my culture, a culture that certainly changed over that length of time. I realize that there are things in this collection that may seem offensive to readers either now or at some unknown time in the future. I stand by the value of these stories aside from cultural trends and changes, and I believe they can speak both to the times of their creation and to universal human issues. I hope some will speak to you!

Dedication

This book is dedicated to you.

Contents

The passage of time is a construct of the human mind.
Eternity is a single moment.
All the words that have ever been
uttered or written are just one letter.

"The Tailor's Confession" won First Prize in Fiction from Crucible *magazine and was published in its Vol. 20, Spring 1984 edition. It was inspired by a homework assignment I did for a class in Spanish I had attended the previous fall. It was the first short story I wrote as an adult and the first to be published.* Crucible *magazine was a non-profit literary magazine, sanctioned and partially supported by Atlantic Christian College, later renamed Barton College.*

The Tailor's Confession

To the Most Pious Brother Tomas de Torquemada,
El Director de Concejo de la Suprema Inquisicion Madrid, Spain

Your Grace,

Your courier arrived at my door this morning with a request for me to come to Madrid to testify at the Tribunal about my association with the Moorish physician, Ibn Hasan, the legendary "Demon of Cordova." I have to report, with deepest regret, that for the last few weeks the stiffness in my legs has grown so painful that I am now forced to spend most of my time in bed. I am sure that you must understand the limitations of the elderly and will permit me to instead dictate my reply to the courier.

I am most certainly, Your Grace, aware of the seriousness of the charges against me, but I am confident that after hearing my story, you will see that I am, in reality, only a simple and unimportant man who has been just a witness to the nightmare that was Cordova just a few years ago.

At that time I worked, as I have always done, in my small tailor shop on the *Camina de Los Sastres*. I have worked hard all my life, struggling day and night just to eke out a living for my little daughter and myself. Although we never had much money, I always gave out of my need to the Church. There never was a Sunday when I didn't attend Mass, except, of course, when my beloved Luisa was too sick to be left alone. It is not in seeking pity, Your Grace, that I tell you these things. It is only to show you that in my home life and my work, I have always tried to follow a life of Christian example. But, yes, it is true that Joseph, my apprentice, was a Jew, but you should have seen how desperate and eager he was when he first came to me for work. When I met him, he was, as he was in the end, a young man of unusual good looks and energy who had arrived in Cordova completely alone in the world and certainly in need of Christian charity. I had always thought he possessed a degree of intelligence, but it was only too late when I came to realize how foolish he really was.

But I am digressing. My mind is not so young any more either, and like a well-worn piece of cloth, it tends occasionally to become unraveled and lose its thread of thought. It is the doctor Ibn Hasan that interests you and your Tribunal. It is strange that so many years and so many miles away, the stories are still told and, with each telling, get a little further and further from the truth. It was the same way in Cordova. When Ibn Hasan first moved into our neighborhood it was said that he was an African Prince who had been banished by his own Moslem people for secretly practicing Christian rituals. Some said he had been a slave trader and others said that he was, himself, an escaped slave. All I knew of him for years was the plain wall that surrounded his home and the small sign that read simply: "Physician."

It is peculiar, Your Grace, how I now can have trouble sometimes remembering where I have put my shoes, yet I can remember the smallest details of years ago. Like the time when I first met Ibn Hasan.

He had come into my shop as I was getting ready to close early one evening at the height of summer with the sunset still lingering in the air. I looked up from my work and saw him for the first time, as I shall always remember him, a dark silhouette standing in my doorway.

It is amusing when I meet someone even now here in Seville, who tells me, all excitedly, how he had once seen Ibn Hasan, how he stood seven feet tall with coal black skin and crimson hair. It is quite something to tell them that, in fact, he was only an average-looking man who had a pleasant face and never had, as far as I know, a fierce glass eye that glowed with the light of a flame.

Although we had never met before that evening, he seemed to know who I was and asked me, in perfect and polite Spanish, if I would make up some coats to his specifications. We talked a little about clothing design, about which he seemed to know a bit, and the only other thing I remember talking about was an unusual gold ring that he wore. It had a snake for a band, and a peacock design on the gem. He told me he bought it many years before when he lived in Constantinople, where, he said, the owner of such a ring was entitled access to certain people and places. And as I stand here in the presence of God, that was all we talked about that night. Of the fighting against the Moors in Granada, or the burning of heretics which was even then taking place in our town, we said nothing, I swear. My world has always been a small one, Your Grace, and my concerns no broader than my family and my shop. I never had, as I do not now, any desire to be involved with affairs which do not concern me.

I imagine it was partly for that reason that I was reluctant to have much to do with Ibn Hasan, and why I decided, several weeks later, to send Joseph over to his home to deliver the finished garments.

Joseph took an unusually long time getting back that day, and though, yes, I was a little concerned, I did not say anything to him about it. You see, I always had a hard time being strict with Joseph. He had a way of using a smile and his sense of humor to charm any anger out of me. But whatever did happen to him that day, whatever strange events occurred, whatever promise or threats he received, I will never know. But it was soon after that when Joseph began to visit regularly the home of Ibn Hasan.

I know it may seem strange to you, Your Grace, that I never asked Joseph about these visits, even when he would do without supper just to get there in time. There were many things about him that I did not know, and though I often found myself praying for his welfare, I tried as best I could not to pry into his affairs. That is why, I suppose, it came as such a surprise to me when I found out about his feeling for my daughter, Luisa.

But, now I am getting ahead of myself. All I knew at that time was that Joseph had taken a new interest in his work, from time to time suggesting ways that we might better organize our work, or make a better tool than what we had been using. In cleaning up his room one night while he was gone, I found some strange drawings. They were really diagrams, I suppose, that he had made of looms and spinning wheels. Now, when I am forced to think back over all these things, I wonder why I never asked him about them when I had the chance.

It was not until Advent of that year that the name of Ibn Hasan was ever spoken again in our home. Luisa and I had returned from Mass one day and she was telling me how she planned to carve some figures for a Nativity scene for the shop window. She was, like her mother, a sensitive and very religious young woman, and went on with great feeling about how she envisioned the Magi, the Virgin, the Christ Child, and Joseph.

It was Joseph, who always spent Sundays working in his room, who was standing in the doorway listening to us discuss the birth of Christ.

"Someday soon," I remember him saying, "there will be machines here in Spain that will print copies of the Bible so quickly that every Spanish Christian will be able to have his own copy. Or her own copy," he said to Luisa.

We just stood in silence. In Cordova, Your Grace, it wasn't considered proper to discuss the Bible with a Jew.

"How do you come to know so much about Bibles and printing machines, Joseph?" I asked, trying as hard as I could to show him my disapproval.

"Master," he said, "I've seen dozens of books that have been printed on machines. Ibn Hasan has told us about them. He saw them printing books when he was in Italy. He has one book from Italy—the diary of an Italian who traveled across the world to Cathay."

"Ibn Hasan! Is that what you do when you go there, look at books?"

His face softened into that smile that somehow disarmed me. "Well, yes," he said. "Sometimes. Sometimes we hear stories about people or places he has been. Sometimes we listen to music and some times," he grinned to me, "we even discuss the art of making clothes."

I reminded him that, speaking of clothes, the only reason I allowed him to observe the Jewish Sabbath on Saturday was that he had always promised to make up his work for me on Sunday. "Besides," I told him, "we have no interest in printing machines here in a tailor shop."

"In France," he said to me, "printing machines are considered tools of the Devil, and we don't want to ever become like the French now, do we?" He left us and I noticed that, for some reason, Luisa was laughing.

It was shortly after this incident I began to find out that several people in Cordova, Christians and Moslems, as well as Jews, met together at the home of Ibn Hasan. I even heard that women were permitted at these meetings, but I have no way of knowing if this was any truer than the stories of the miraculous healings.

No, I'm terribly sorry, Your Grace, if I ever heard the names of the individuals who attended those meetings, they have been lost forever in the warp and woof of my memory.

All I remember is that by Christmas of that year I thought that things had never been better. My shop had never been as prosperous, in part thanks to the intercession of the Blessed Virgin, and in part thanks to the changes Joseph and I had made in our work. But how little I really knew! How foolish and vain of me to forget that goodness is never secured merely by prosperity. But I soon came to understand though, when 1491 became 1492 our world began to change.

That year! Even now I find myself waking in the middle of the night, trembling, and afraid it is 1492 again. The days grew longer as winter wore on, but it was as if the light never returned to Cordova that spring. Oh, we heard the news from Granada, how Ferdinand had finally conquered the Moors, but that joy was distant. Much closer to us was the fear—the fear that hung in the air like gloom and rain as the Inquisition tightened its grip on the citizens of Cordova. Twice that winter we were awakened during the night by the screams of our neighbors being taken away for questioning. Twice Luisa and I were questioned as to why we had not been the ones to turn them in. Were we trying to protect anyone? I never knew them. I never spoke to them. I closed the windows to my home and never thought to look through my neighbor's. How were we to know who had not been born Christian, and how would we know if they had lapsed into some kind of heresy? Those people, whose voices still echo in my mind, were never seen again. I saw widows and children, torn away from their crying families. But, I suppose, there is no need to go into any of this. The activities of the Inquisition in Cordova must all be somewhere on record. It is only the feelings, Your Grace, the feelings that filled our every public move and every private moment that no record could ever contain.

It was March of that year, while we walked with our eyes to the ground for fear of betraying an unwitting look of guilt or accusation, that I again saw the doctor Ibn Hasan. For the first time in more than half a year, Joseph had missed his regular Thursday night visit to the home of the Moor, and it was to this that I attributed the arrival of the man who was called "The Demon of Cordova."

When he entered the shop, or how long he had been watching me work there on the floor I didn't know, but I felt a presence and turned to see him standing over me. He must have been some time in the rain that dismal day, since his cloak and hair and even his gold ring were wet with cold droplets. I even thought for a minute that his face was stained with teardrops, but if he had been feeling any emotion, he did not show it in his voice when we began talking about tailoring and the design of clothes. He started to tell me about a group of Spanish tailors he knew who lived in Constantinople, going into the most extraordinary detail about their names and where they lived, and how he still heard from them through the ships that sailed to and from there from Seville.

Finally, I must have shown some impatience with what I thought to be an irrelevant travelogue, because he suddenly changed the tone of his voice and brought out a thin paper package from a pocket under his cloak. "Please give this to Joseph for me," he told me. "It is very important."

Well, I started to go into the back to find Joseph and let the two settle their own business without involving me, but the Moor disappeared before I knew it. Yes, Your Grace, I did give Joseph the package that same day, but I was not there when he opened it. I never had a chance to ask him about it because it was only a day or two after that when we heard the Edict of Exile. We could not understand at first why the King would order all Jews to leave Spain by that summer. For what crimes? We never heard. But we did hear how Jewish property in Cordova was being confiscated. How a house was sold for only a few *pesadas* to pay off a debt. How the Jewish cemetery across town was being plowed into pasture land. It was that same week, when events seemed to follow each other like patches on a jester's coat, that Joseph told me he wished to become a Christian, and it was then, Your Grace, that he asked for the hand of my daughter in marriage.

What could I say? I had never wanted a Jew for a son-in-law, even such a converted one. And what a time for a marriage! But what could I do? They stood there in front of me telling me how long they had been in love and that they wanted to be married as soon as they could. I do not mind telling you that I could not keep myself from crying when Luisa held my hand and told me how wonderful it would be, that someday she and Joseph would take over care of the shop. I told them I was crying for the joy of the two young people I loved so much, but even then, I believe, somehow I sensed the tragedy that lay in wait for those innocent souls.

But I tried not to show my fears. In all modesty, I have to admit that the dress that Luisa wore in the wedding was probably my finest, and most certainly my fastest work. Within a week Joseph had been baptized and he and Luisa were married. Father Francesco performed both sacraments. We have no family, Your Grace, and it was a small Mass, held on a cold, wet morning with only a few of our neighbors as witnesses. I could not take my eyes off my beautiful daughter, standing there in a gown, sewn with fingers trembling with emotion. It was only as we were leaving Church I saw the men standing in the shadows behind the last pew. They wore the black robes of the Inquisition and watched us with empty, soulless eyes. I shivered from the damp wind and made the sign of the Cross.

But how we celebrated that night! It was as if time held its breath for us for one evening. We ate and ate and drank until Joseph got drunk, although I often remember him swearing he never would do so. We talked for hours about life and children and love, about Luisa's mother, about Joseph's hopes and dreams. But never did we talk about Ibn Hasan, or books, or packages, or the duties of a Christian life. And when we could not talk anymore, I hugged and kissed them both and told Joseph he must take Luisa out to the country to a certain inn I knew, where, so many years before, I spent my own wedding night. Usually I am a very abstemious man and getting on so much in years now, that I am afraid I suffered the next day for my indulgences. In fact, I felt so ill that I decided only to clean up a little to make a nice place for the two of them to come home to. I certainly did not mean to pry, it was only that, in the trash, I could not help but see the torn remains of the package left for Joseph by Ibn Hasan. Why did I bother to look inside? Why did I think to take the contents out and put them away in my chest? I do not know. Maybe it was because, as I said, I was not myself that day and not thinking clearly. But once again, I will swear to God that is the reason that when Your Inquisitors later searched my house they found in my chest passage for two persons to Italy, passports, and a Letter of Introduction. They were not mine, Your Grace, they belonged to Joseph.

At first I was furious at Ibn Hasan for giving Joseph these things. Obviously he had intended for Joseph to take my daughter away and leave the country. Had Joseph asked for them? If he had, then why did he throw them away? I had no answers. But there was something else with the package, something that the Inquisitors never found. It was a small note that said something like this: "My dear Joseph, when you took on the responsibility of being my student, you undertook a journey the end of which you could not foresee. My responsibility has been to try to help you even at the risk of being rebuffed or misunderstood. The plans we discussed are necessary not only for your welfare, but for the continuation of our Work. If, on the other hand, you feel you have to follow your own course, you will have to accept the consequences and, God willing, you will be given a chance to learn from this. In any event, I doubt we shall see each other in this life again. I pray for your soul. Signed Ibn Hasan."

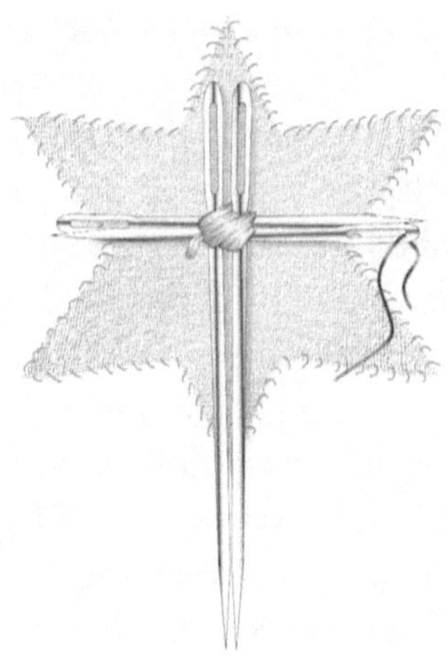

The prayers of Ibn Hasan did not save Joseph. Neither did mine. It was the middle of the night when they came to get him. I was asleep when a cold breeze blew suddenly through the house followed by a thunder of heavy feet. I sat up in bed with my heart going wild. Luisa screamed and I came out of my room in time to see them dragging my two children down the dark stairway. I tried to run after them, but tripped, fell and twisted my legs. I was paralyzed for a moment, unable to do anything but lie there in the dark, helpless even to reach my own pleading daughter.

The scene is vivid to me even now. I have relived it so many times in my dreams. It is strange, though, that when I fell I was too frightened to feel any pain, and it has only been in the years since that the chronic pain I now suffer has more than made up for the moment of my injury.

I never did discover what actually happened that night. I suspect that you know much more about it than I ever will. But somehow, I know in my heart, that whoever was my daughter Luisa died that night. The young girl who returned home the next morning, alone, was just a shadow without a soul. She would not say anything to me, just pushed me aside with a limp hand and climbed the stairs to her room.

It was a neighbor, finally, a person I hardly knew, who told me later that it had been reported to the Inquisition that Joseph had been seen working on a Sunday. Yes, it probably was true! But if it was, it was my fault and not his. He had been a Christian for only a few weeks and had spent years before that as a Jew working for me on Sunday. If I complained about our work being behind schedule, I never meant for him to do anything sacrilegious. We never thought after so long to discuss with him the Christian life. But why? He had accepted Christ with his baptism. Wasn't that enough?

After a few days I became desperate with concern for my daughter. She refused to eat and soon grew too weak to get out of bed. In the meantime we heard nothing from the Tribunal. One man who had been a customer of mine for years sent me a note through a stranger telling me he was afraid to come into my shop and asking if I could deliver his shirts to him after dark. When I did so later he told me he had heard that

Joseph had been convicted of heresy and had, under torture, implicated everyone he knew. Would we ever see him again? He did not know.

Luisa grew worse. I went to Father Francesco, begging him to come help us. All he gave were his regrets. Would he at least come and give her communion? He said he was afraid to come into my house, and I never knew if it was in fear of the laws of God or the laws of the Inquisition. When I asked him, in God's Name, to pray for her, he turned his eyes away from mine and said, "I am sorry."

What else was there for me to do? I didn't know anyone in Cordova with medical knowledge other than the priest. And, yes, I knew it was against the law for a Moslem doctor to treat a Christian, but I ask you, what was I to do? Do you know how a man who has nothing in his life but his love for his daughter will take any kind of risk? Do you know how risks become less and less important as his desperation increases? The next day I decided to go to ask help from Ibn Hasan.

I left early in the morning when I was sure Luisa was asleep and walked through the empty streets to the white stucco wall that surrounded the home of Ibn Hasan. It surprised me, when, almost as soon as I had rung the bell, the door was opened by a man I took to be a servant, dressed in a clean, white tunic.

"I have come to see Doctor Ibn Hasan," I told him, "to throw myself on his mercy, to plead with him . . ." but before I could say any more, the man turned and motioned me to enter. I have to tell you, Your Grace, that what I saw behind the gate was unlike anything I have ever seen or hope to see again until, God willing, I am allowed into Christ's own Mansion.

Behind the wall was a luxurious garden, very fragrant there in the morning air and full of flowers which looked like they had come from Eden itself. An alabaster fountain flowed with silvery water that collected in small pools. I was led down a short path, through an archway into an open room of fresh blue and white walls with a soft carpet on the floor. Every thing I saw gleamed with such immaculate cleanliness that I began to feel ashamed for myself, and I thought how meager and shabby my own home must appear to the owner of such a place as this.

I heard his voice. "There is nothing more I can do for Joseph. All that has been possible has already been done." He entered the room followed by a man carrying tea on a silver tray. "Please sit down," he said to me and when I looked at him I, for some reason, became afraid that he knew that I had read his letter to Joseph.

"It isn't for Joseph that I come," I told him, hearing my own voice becoming weak. "I've come to you to ask you to help—to plead with you to come and help her—Luisa, Joseph's wife— my daughter" I am ashamed to admit that I threw myself down on my injured knees in front of this man, this unbaptized heathen, who was at that moment my only hope in the world.

He lifted me up, set me on a divan and gave me a cup of tea. Neither one of us said anything about the law which forbid him to attend to a Christian patient though both of us knew it. Neither one of us said anything about Joseph's confession and his betrayal, although we both suspected it. But somehow, thanks to God's mercy at that moment, it did not matter.

After I had regained some of my composure, he asked me to follow him into the next room where he kept his medicines. There in the dim light and pungent smells I saw his books, row after row, which covered an entire wall. Across from the books were shelves filled with colored glass jars that gleamed like jewels in the lamplight. I watched him take a plain metal box from a drawer and fill it thoughtfully with herbs and potions that he chose according to his own foreign science. I felt there in the dark as if I had stumbled into a world in which I did not belong and suddenly was afraid to be alone there with such a powerful and mysterious person.

"There really is not much time," he said turning to me. "Now in payment for my services I would like you to make me a few plain, warm cloaks, nothing complicated or elaborate. I will need them today." I simply stared at him dumbly. "We had better be going," he told me and took his box and my arm and led me back through the garden into the street.

When we reached my shop, he went straightway up to Luisa's room and, when I asked what I could do to help, he just mentioned to me again about the cloaks. I tell you it was difficult to concentrate on work, not knowing what was going on upstairs. At noon I stopped for lunch and went quietly to see. Ibn Hasan was sitting by her bed, holding one of her hands and talking to her so softly that I could not hear what he was saying. At three I was interrupted by the sounds of Luisa crying. I rushed upstairs in a panic but the Moor motioned me out with his hand. I stood there outside the door fighting my feelings of anger and concern for a moment until I realized it was the first time I had heard her cry since they had taken Joseph away. I am just a father, not a physician, but I decided it was best for me not to interfere.

It was dark before he came downstairs and asked me to take Luisa some soup. I saw that he carried his box with him and for a moment I was going to ask him not to leave us. Instead, I just gave him what I had done of the cloaks and asked, "Will you come back?"

"*Inshallah*," he said to me in Arabic. "If God wills."

That night, after Luisa had taken some soup we talked for a little while. It was the first time I had heard her voice in so long, the first time I had seen light in her eyes. We talked for a while, not about Joseph or Ibn Hasan, but about days long before, those happy days when she was a young child. There were things that I had completely forgotten, but that she remembered vividly, and for one evening my daughter had returned from the dead.

I sat there as the candle burned beside her bed, praying for her to fall asleep. Finally, much later, my own capacity for worry ran out and I drifted off there in the chair, dreaming fitfully that I had become trapped in Hell. I saw myself in a burning pit, surrounded by taunting demons. Unable to move, I fell on my knees in prayer. Suddenly Christ himself appeared before me and opened one of the walls to show me what at first I thought to be the New Jerusalem, a city that shone with Oriental spires touched by clouds. It was not Jerusalem, it was Constantinople.

I jerked awake and for a moment thought that I was still dreaming, I could still smell the burning smoke. But somehow, for a reason that I can not explain, I knew all at once what was happening. I ran to the window and saw the haze of smoke drifting through the streets in the gray dawn.

My legs, you know, were still hurting, so it was painful even to take the stairs, but I ignored the stabbing and ran wildly out of the house and down the streets to where I prayed I should not have to see what I knew I would. There they were, neighbors and friends, the good people of Cordova, screaming and shouting in a mob around the burning home of Ibn Hasan. "Demon, demon, demon," was their litany as they heaved torches over the blackened wall,

There is no way that I will ever be able to explain to you, Your Grace, how I felt or what were my thoughts as I stood there among them that morning. It was then that I understood something I had never known. Something that I could never make anyone understand who has not been behind the fragile curtain which hides the animal in us. It was then, for the first time, that I understood the sin in the soul that neither Baptism nor all the Sacraments can erase. I saw it all as I watched them, wearing clothes that I myself had made, the faces that I knew better than my own, transformed into shouting, braying beasts.

But heaven has mercy even on the beasts, and at last, through the clouds of smoke a cold rain began to fall and the flames died down into the fog and steam. They rushed into the smoldering ruins, carrying me with them in their frantic tide, searching the bodies of their victims. And when, as everyone knows, there were no bodies to be found, no trace of anyone at all, the crowd went wild and, in their frustration began to smash anything they could.

As for me, I wandered through the smoke and ashen grave of what just the day before had been a paradise and found myself in the room that had been the laboratory of Ibn Hasan. I think that even then, choking and coughing from smoke, I hoped against hope to find something to help us. The books still burned and the glass jars, smashed and empty, sizzled as the rain fell through the open roof. There it was, in the rubble, the metal box of Ibn Hasan, covered with ashes that, as I brushed them away, revealed a name plainly etched across the top. My name.

I burned my hand trying to open it. Inside there were no medicines, no potions, no answers, only the ring, the gold ring from Constantinople. I put it in my pocket and left the box where it was later found by your agents, Your Grace.

And that is all I knew of Ibn Hasan. He was searched for, but neither he nor his friends were ever found. It was two weeks after he disappeared when Luisa died. Without the medicines of Ibn Hasan, without his counsel, without any word from Joseph, without hope, she died in her sleep. The church would not have her, so I buried her one night under the ruins of the garden of Ibn Hasan, beside the alabaster fountain.

They came shortly after, as you know, and seized my shop as payment for Joseph's trial. It came to me as a relief. It was as if everything in my life, my home, my shop, my town, had become tainted with an awful sickness which had nearly destroyed us all. I could not bear to live there anymore, so in the fall of that year, I moved to Seville where I now work by the docks making sails for those great ships that carry the glory of Spain across the seas. Even though I now am alone, even though there are times when I am not able, I still try to work hard, saving up my money for—well, for someday.

I hope that my story will satisfy the Tribunal, every word is the truth, I swear. But, whatever should be your decision, please remember that my days here are numbered in any event, and that an old man like myself is never far from the Judgment that comes to us all.

But here in Seville, the talk is not about Guilt or Innocence, nor about Jew nor Moslem, but rather about exploration and discovery. Here in town is the famous Italian Admiral, Cristobal Colon, who has just returned from his second trip to those Indian Islands he had discovered. I watched them come into port last fall with their cargo of brown slaves. For some reason the sailors looked ill and disturbed, as if they had witnessed some great tragedy. The Admiral himself now goes about Seville, dressed in sackcloth like a mourner.

Please do not misunderstand. It is, of course, with a deep sense of pride in our Country and King that I serve these mighty ships of discovery. It's just something, Your Grace, something that I cannot quite explain, something which tugs at me when I sit and watch the tall ships glide off toward the sea. It is something which makes me look away and pray to God that, wherever those ships are going, they will not carry with them this awful sickness.

Yours in Christ,

Pablo Sacado el Sastre de Cordova,
December 23, 1496

"Strangers" won the prize for Best Short Story by Sucarnochee Review, *the Spring 1987 edition.* Sucarnochee Review *is a publication of Livingston University, renamed Western Alabama University in Livingston, Alabama. It was inspired by a play consisting of short scenes from cartoons by Jules Feiffer. I believe the play might have been* Feiffer's People.

Strangers

If there's one thing that grown-ups can't handle, it's death. I've seen my mother a stone-faced martyr, I've seen her a cold-hearted bitch, but I never saw her in weepy hysterics until the day my grandfather died. My old man, too, acted like a complete jackass, hanging around the house, yelling at us to keep quiet, like he thought that was going to make Mom feel better. But for me death is no big deal. I mean, the sooner I get out of here, the better I'll like it. And I don't just mean this crummy town either. I mean the whole damn planet.

It doesn't take a genius to figure it out. You come into this world screaming and crying, and you grow up just in time to find out that life stinks. Then, before you can do anything about it, you turn old and decrepit, and that's the end of it. For me, I think it should be different. Don't ask me why. Pop calls me a spoiled brat, but he never has time to think about stuff like this, being too busy worrying over the bills, and if we can afford a new car and more clothes for Mom. But I say, who cares?

Well, the thing is, practically everybody does except me. I guess that's why I spend a lot of time by myself. It's not that I'm a loner or think I'm better than anybody else. I'm just different. I guess you could say that I'm sort of a person of mystery and secrets.

As far back as I can remember I've been different. My whole life I've had crazy dreams at night, not that I ever told anybody about them. They'd probably say it was because I read too many books, but I had those dreams even before I could talk. But what's really strange is how even now something will happen and make me remember them as clear as if it were happening all over again.

Take the time when we went to see Grandpop in the hospital. Right off I knew something big was up, because all of us went, even Pop, who called Grandpop "that old coot," and used to say he needed about three lobotomies just to make him normal. I didn't know him too well, myself, since Pop thought he was a bad influence on us and wouldn't let him in the house.

Now, I'm old enough to go up into the hospital part, but Amy and Jeffery aren't, so I was volunteered to stay with them down in the lobby. I didn't mind too much, being pretty sure that Mom didn't want me to see her go berserk when she saw Grandpop lying there with tubes up his ass, or whatever it is that people look like just before they die.

After about five minutes I realized there wasn't too much to do down there except look through some magazines, mostly old copies of *Consumer's Digest*, which didn't hold my interest too long. My tastes in reading, as everybody knows, go more

24

toward science fiction and fantasy. In fact, I don't think there's a book in the whole sci-fi section of the school library that doesn't have my fingerprints all over it. Mom says she can't figure out why I don't do better at school since I like to read so much, but what she doesn't know is that all that crap we're supposed to read is about life on the planet Earth, and like I said, I'm just not interested.

So, after making Jeffery promise not to pound Amy on the head, I decided to cut out for a while and told them I had to go to the bathroom. Instead, I went outside to have a smoke. I usually keep a cigarette rolled up in some aluminum foil in my inside jacket pocket just for times like that. I lit up and took a drag.

It was kind of late in the day, and there were lots of cars going around in the parking lot, and I started thinking it would be just my luck for one of Mom's friends to be on her way into the hospital for a face lift or something, and see me out there smoking and, bam, there would go my chances for getting a telescope for Christmas. So I boosted myself up on the wall outside the parking lot, walked around behind the hospital to make sure I was out of sight, and sat down where I could look all the way up to Montgomery Avenue. I knew that everybody from school was probably up at the Greek's. I don't hang out there myself much anymore, not that anybody would miss me. Pinky Detweiller might miss me, but that's only because I was nice to her once after Gregg Miller called her a fat douche bag. I get a lot of crap from everybody for ever being nice to her, but I couldn't care less. Those guys aren't real friends. Not like the Bird People were to Olor of Cygnus in *Flights of Destiny.*

It started to get cold so I chucked my butt and went to head back. When I stood up on the wall I could see that the sun was just going down over the train station, and the hospital and the parking lot and the street were covered with this eerie gold light that kind of froze everything like a Polaroid picture. All of a sudden it made me think about those dreams I used to have, like I said, when I was a kid. It was like I could remember standing there just like that some other time, only I couldn't remember when. I sort of had this feeling that something was going to happen. Don't ask me to explain it because I can't. Not even if I wanted to.

By the time I made it back to the lobby, Pop was down there looking for me, but instead of being mad and yelling, he just told me to go up to Grandpop's room. I took the elevator on up, and let me tell you, if ever there was a room where somebody was dying, it was this one. The room was about completely dark and quiet, except for this machine that sounded like when you leave the phone off the hook. Mom was just where I thought she'd be, in the corner going to pieces while a man in a white coat patted her on the shoulder. I figured he was either an undertaker or a scout from the mental ward, either way, waiting around for some new business.

Grandpop turned his head when I came in. He didn't look too good, which was just about right under the circumstances, but then again I can't say I knew what he was supposed to look like either, because I never did know him too well. You might say we were practically strangers.

Mom always told us he was jolly and loved practical jokes, but Pop just said he was goofy. Well, he didn't seem too goofy or too jolly at the moment, but he did look at me and move his mouth like he was saying "Michael." Since that's my name, I figured he must have meant me, so I kind of sauntered on over to his bed.

I wasn't quite sure what to say to him, so we both just looked each other over for a moment, me hoping he wasn't going to make me promise on his deathbed to give up smoking or something. He pulled out a bony white hand from under the covers and sort of waved it around, and after a second I got the idea that he wanted me to pull up the shade on the window.

The man in white was looking at his watch, and I couldn't see any reason not to, so I gave the thing a yank, and the last of the daylight poured in over the old man 's bed. He smiled at me, and I saw that he was lit up by that same gold light I had seen outside. For some reason I started to get scared.

I watched as the light seemed to fill up in his eyes, and I had a feeling something was going on. There was something about that old man's face that made me think of all those dreams, and they all rushed into my mind like I was getting dizzy. I knew I had seen that exact same face before in my dreams.

Then the busy sound stopped, and the man in white rushed over and pushed a button, and about twenty people swooped in and took Grandpop away, and that's the last I ever saw of him. And I'm really sorry because there's a lot now I'd like to talk to him about.

*   *   *

I guess a couple of weeks was all Pop could take, because it was just about that long after the funeral that he left to go to Detroit. He said it was a business trip, but I knew it was mostly to get away from Mom's idiotic behavior for a while. It was getting where she couldn't get up the energy to cook even a half-decent meal for us, and if it wasn't for me and my famous spaghetti, I think we all might have starved to death.

It was just about then that Grandpop's lawyer kept calling all the time, bitching how he had to sell Grandpop's house, and if we wanted anything out of there we'd better get it in a hurry or he'd get some colored guys and have it all hauled off to the dump. And with Pop out of town and Mom staying in her pajamas all day, it looked like you might as well could write off whatever Grandpop had left here on Earth.

Normally I couldn't have cared less about the whole thing. It was only that something about that old man kept coming up in my mind.

Two nights after Pop left, I had another dream. I'm climbing up these dark stairs, and suddenly I see Grandpop standing up at the top in a space helmet and he says to me, "Hello, Michael."

I start thinking this is crazy. "You're supposed to be dead," I say and he laughs and starts to walk away.

"I'm going back home now," he says. "I want you to look through what I've left behind." And out of nowhere he climbs into a flying saucer.

"Is this a dream or what?" I holler, but I just hear him laughing as he blasts off into Outer Space, and I start bawling, wishing I was on that saucer, too.

The next morning I tried to get that dream out of my head, but I couldn't. So by the middle of fourth period I decided that I was just going to have to do something about it. The only thing was, I was pretty sure that Mom wouldn't like the idea of me going over to Grandpop's house by myself, and there was no way she'd go with me now that her butt had gotten frozen to the sofa. So it looked like I'd have to handle it like a secret mission, like when Malik of Roterra had to bust into thc Temple of Mystery to recover the power source for the Andromeda Galaxy. The only thing was, Malik had help from the Guardians of the Universe. The only help I got was from Pinky Detweiller.

Pinky had come up to me at lunch and asked if I was feeling okay and how my family was since she knew my grandfather had died. I told her that, if she really wanted to know, some guys from Hollywood were coming over to make a disaster movie at our house. And when she asked if there was anything she could do to help, I said, "Sure, you can help me break into my grandfather's house and get his valuables out before they're trashed," just sort of being sarcastic. But she said, sure, she'd love to. I was surprised at first, not thinking that somebody like Pinky would want to go on a risky mission like that. Later I guessed it was probably because she had the hots for me, and that's the way girls can be about those things.

So after breakfast Saturday I got Pop's toolbox out of the basement and took a hammer and a couple of screwdrivers and wrapped them in a sweatshirt and told Mom I was going over to Steve Hoft's to play darts and make a few phony phone calls.

I met Pinky behind the Greek's, and we rode our bikes over to the Blood Bank, which is what Pop calls the liquor store, and got as many boxes as we could pile on and managed to get most of them out to Garret Hill, a couple of blocks past that pizza place that burned down, which is where Grandpop's house was. I hadn't been there in a long time, and for some reason it didn't look as big as I remembered it, but it might have been because the last time I was in it I had been a lot smaller.

We stashed our bikes behind some garbage cans in the back and brought the boxes and tools up to the back door.

"Well?" said Pinky like she didn't think I knew what I was doing.

"I know what I'm doing," I said.

"You're going to have to open the door from the inside like they do on TV," she said.

Well, I'm not too up on most of what they do on TV, except for maybe Star Trek or Sci-fi Theatre, but I took the screwdrivers out of the sweatshirt and stuck one of them in the lock.

"No, not like that, Michael. Don't you know anything?" She grabbed up the hammer and put the sweatshirt up on a pane of glass and started tapping until the whole thing shattered. Then she reached her hand in, and the door popped open.

"I hope your Grandfather doesn't care you had to break his back door," she said.

The switch inside didn't work. It was dark and reeked of the smell an old man makes when he's sick, but Pinky went right on in, pulled the curtains, and opened a window.

For a small house there was an awful lot of junk in it. Not even Jeffrey's bedroom on a bad day ever had as much stuff as was strewn around in there. It didn't look like he had bothered to clean up before he left, which I wouldn't have done either, if I knew I was going to die before I had to come back.

"Why is it that men can never straighten up after themselves?" asked Pinky like I was supposed to give her an answer. She picked up a book from off the floor and started thumbing through it. "Where was your grandfather from, Michael?"

I told her I couldn't remember anybody ever saying.

"I don't think it was from America," she said.

I went back outside for just a second to get the boxes and by the time I got back she had already started poking around, pulling open drawers and sticking her hands into cupboards. The way she did it kind of bugged me. It seemed a little rude or something. So I asked her if she had never heard that rats liked to make their homes in the drawers in houses of dead people.

But she didn't answer me and kept nosing around, eyeballing the bottoms of old glasses and the handles of silverware like she was looking for a big find.

"You better start boxing things up, Michael," she said to me in a way that made me wonder who had made her the boss. "I'm going to see if I can find the key to that china closet." Of course that gave me the raw end of the deal, but I decided not to say anything about it.

The only thing was, I wasn't too sure what I was supposed to be boxing up. There was an awful lot of stuff to choose from. Over the fireplace were six clocks, a couple of radios, and a painting of a place with a red and yellow sky. There were bookshelves with little statues and about a hundred old pictures all over the walls. The people in the pictures didn't look like anyone I knew or would ever want to know. Except for one picture of Mom as a little girl looking so nerdy, I felt a little sorry for her, and it made me wonder if she got as much shit when she was in school as Pinky Detweiller.

Pinky finally found some old keys, none of which fit the china closet, and by that time I had boxed up some of the statues and one of the clocks that looked like it might have had some gold in it. I felt like the whole mission was turning out to be a big bust, and I was ready to bag it, but Pinky kept wanting to go and see what was upstairs. I told her there wasn't much point in it, and besides, it was pretty dark upstairs and the lights didn't work.

"Are you scared?" she said. I thought it sounded like one of the stupidest questions I had ever heard.

"No," I said.

"Well, let's go," she said. And up she went.

Even though I wasn't at all scared, there was something about the shadow that the railing made on the wall that bothered me. It looked just like the entrance to the Secret Vault on the cover of Planets of Mystery.

I heard Pinky let out a kind of squeal, just the sort of thing that Gregg Miller would say made her sound like a pig. "Michael, come look! A canopy bed."

I followed her into the bedroom. It was just about as slobbed out as the rest of the house. "Don't you think that canopy beds are the most romantic thing?" she asked me, plopping down on the quilt. I hoped she didn't think I was going to start making out with her. Even though she's not too bad, she's a little too chubby for my tastes and besides, she chews her fingernails.

"I wouldn't sit there if I were you," I warned her, reaching to pull her up. "There are probably billions of my Grandpop's germs all over that quilt."

She just kind of pushed me aside and made a beeline out the door. "What do you think's in this room, Michael?" she called from the hall.

I asked her what made her think I knew. "It's locked," she said.

I went back out in the dark hallway and found her twiddling the knob on the door by the stairs. I was starting to get one of my funny feelings. Pinky pulled out the keys that wouldn't open the china closet and fished through about five or six, and sure enough, one of them opened the door.

"You go first," she said. "It's your grandfather's house."

I didn't want to, but I pushed the door open.

"Goddamn," was all I could say.

I mean, how can I describe it? It looked like a planetarium

or something. It was just a little room, but painted all black with little white stars. There were star maps on the walls and model rockets hanging from the ceiling, and even a silver space suit. But the most unbelievable thing of all was an old telescope set up on a stand next to the window, just looking up at the sky.

"What's all this?" said Pinky, shoving her way in. She gave the room the once over. "What was your grandfather, an astronaut, or what?"

I had to touch the telescope to make sure it was real. It was. "I don't know what he was."

She went over to the space suit. "If your grandfather wasn't an astronaut, why would he have all this stuff around?" Her eyes started popping out of her skull. "Michael," she said, grabbing at my sleeve, "maybe your Grandfather was really an alien!"

I got a cold shiver down my back. "What do you mean?" My voice kind of cracked.

"I've seen it on TV. Beings from another world come down to Earth and live with human beings, and no one suspects that they're really illegal aliens. Until after they die, when somebody comes and destroys all the evidence. Think about it!"

Well at first I didn't know what to think. It seemed pretty incredible. But when I started thinking about everything — the old man's face, the planetarium, the scope and those dreams— it all began to make a little sense. Everything started to come together, just like when Olor of Cygnus left the Planet of the Duck People, and looked into the Mirror of Truth at the end of *Flights of Destiny* and found out he was really the Prince of the Swan People.

34

"Pinky Detweiller," I whispered so low I could hardly hear myself. She looked at me, and I looked at her, and we both sat there looking at each other. I took her hand, and I put it on my heart. "Do you solemnly swear to keep this a secret for as long as we both shall live?" Her eyes started looking wet, and in a second she was acting blubbery. "Oh, Michael. Oh, Michael," she sobbed and reached over and kissed me on the mouth. I took it that meant yes.

* * *

So that's all I know about the whole thing. I decided to leave all the clocks and stuff behind. Pinky and I took the telescope down, wrapped it in a blanket, and put it in a box. I did stick in the picture of Mom just to fill up a little left over space. I got it home all right and set up the scope in my bedroom. I said I got it from Steve Hoft's brother, which is a big joke on everybody because Steve Hoft doesn't even have a brother.

When Pop got home and saw it, he raised a big stink because he thought I was going to use it to spy on the neighbors. But Mom somehow talked him into letting me keep it, and she even went out and bought me a couple of books on astronomy.

Last weekend I went back up to Garret Hill, but there was a big pick-up full of trash in Grandpop's driveway and a FOR SALE sign in the front lawn. Over the back door was a piece of plastic. For a while I was kind of sad about it, but I'm over it now.

Oh, I'm doing all right. I still have a lot of crazy dreams. Some of them are nice, but sometimes they wake me up so bad I can't get back to sleep, no matter how hard I try. But I don't sweat it anymore. Nowadays I'll just get out of bed, and if it's a clear night, I'll sit down at the scope and check out the sky.

And, you know, after a while I start feeling pretty good, just looking at all those stars and thinking about where I belong.

*I was waiting for a doctor's appointment once and
the receptionist was either overly bored or overly
friendly and told me more about her personal life than
I expected. This wasn't her story, but it started me
thinking about all the meanings of the title word.*

*It was probably written in early 2006 and published in the
now defunct* ESC! Magazine *in their Spring 2007 edition.*

*I did travel once to Boston to see a girl with
whom I thought I was in love. It didn't go much
better than it did for the receptionist.*

Reception

"It will be just a few minutes. Doctor Swankowski's running a little behind this morning. No, don't sit down yet, Mr. Ferguson. May I call you Robert? You know some people named Robert want you to call them Rob, and some like Bob. I think Bob sounds more friendly, don't you, Bob?

"Well, here you go. You have to fill out this form. Make sure you answer all the questions, but you can skip the one about if you are pregnant. Well, unless you are, of course. That's just a joke. Some people might not think something like that was funny—a joke about a man being pregnant. You never know about who's touchy about what these days. There was a guy on the radio yesterday that said that the government is going to outlaw people from saying 'God bless you' after a person sneezes because of separation of church and state. Can you believe that?

"Well I don't believe it. I think they make up that stuff on talk radio just to get people riled up. As for me, I think that most people are already too riled up. I'd rather listen to that station that plays the music from the eighties and nineties, but it comes in with too much static. Do you like eighties and nineties music, Bob? You look like you might be too old for eighties and nineties music. You look more like you like music from the sixties. Am I right? You know you don't have to be embarrassed about your age. It's something that you have to put down on the form anyway.

"No, that's the only pen I've got. I'm sorry it's so chewed up. That's just a nervous habit of mine. I have a lot of energy. It just gets built up since I have to spend so much time just sitting. What I think I'd really like to do is have a job where I could be more active. That's why I'm overweight. Yes, I really am. That's nice of you to say, but you haven't seen me standing up. See? Look at my ankles. I guess you can't see through the window, but my ankles are really puffy. My mother used to tell me that I had permanent water weight gain. I don't think there is such a thing, do you?

"I'd really like to have long, skinny legs but I guess some things you just have to learn to like about yourself. I'll bet you don't like the fact that your hair is so thin, Bob, but there's not much you can do about it. Maybe there's a cream that would help, I don't know. I've never needed to grow hair, mostly I have to try to stop hair from growing. Like on my fat legs and other places. God, it's so embarrassing for me to wear a bikini. I have to use a depilatory. Do you know what that is? Most men don't.

"I started shaving my legs when I was twelve. My mother made me do it. She said that no boy would ever want to date a girl whose legs were hairier than his. I used to shave my legs every other day, but I never did get many dates in high school. Only one, really.

"Would you like a cup of coffee, Bob? Are you sure? Okay, I hope you don't mind if I have one. Drinking coffee helps me to relax. Isn't that funny? Most people say that coffee peps them up. It just goes to show how different people can be.

"So my mom sent me to a psychologist when I was sixteen. Barbara—that was the psychologist—she told me that I needed to learn to like myself the way I was. She said I had low self-esteem. I don't know if she was right or not. I only went one time. I think it was a free introductory lesson. I'm not sure.

"So Barbara asked me if there was any boy in school that I liked, and I said, sure I liked all the cute ones, like Jason O'Dell. He was like the most popular kid in school. Then she said I should go up to Jason and talk to him. Well, that idea was so embarrassing it made me feel like I was going to pee in my pants. Really. You might not believe me but it's true.

"So then I said Norman Geckle because he was a boy I thought I could go up and talk to. He sat next to me in Biology and he let me copy his notes once after I had been sick. I think I had had diarrhea or something. I can't remember, but I do remember that he gave me his notes and he smiled a lot, even though his teeth weren't that good. So Barbara—that was the psychologist—she made me promise her that I'd ask Norman to do something, like outside of school. So I did.

"Would you like me to change the radio station? The doctor doesn't like it when the news is on out here. He says it can upset people. I don't know if it does or not. Sometimes when I hear the President, I wonder if he has good self-esteem. I would think you would have to or you wouldn't be president, don't you? Oh, I wish I could get in that station that plays the eighties and nineties music. I really like Sheryl Crowe. I think it's so sad about her cancer. But we get people with cancer in here all the time. You just never can tell looking at someone, unless their hair is coming out. It's all so sad.

"So I called Norman on the phone, and he wanted to know if I needed his Biology notes again. I think that was a joke. I was so nervous! I could feel trickles running down my arms. Have you ever felt that way, Bob? I guess everyone has at one time or another. I would have hung up right there and then except that Barbara had made me promise her that I would do it.

"I asked him if he would come with me and my family to my cousin's wedding at the Oakcrest Country Club and he said, sure because he had always wanted to go to the Oakcrest Country Club. Well, at first it was a big relief that he had said he would, but then I thought how I would actually have to go on a quote-unquote date with him and actually see him at school knowing we were going on a quote-unquote date. And it was weird, not because it was any different at school, but because it wasn't any different at all. I guess I thought it might be like we were boy and girlfriend. To be honest, I really did think it would be like that, but it wasn't.

"Oh, I'm just going to put the radio on that country station. I hate country music. Don't you? I think just about everybody hates country music. But still, the reception is so good. That's why I listen to it.

"So my mom had to pick him up. My dad wouldn't go since my cousin was my cousin on my mom's side. The wedding was at the Presbyterian Church, even though my cousin's not a Presbyterian. I don't even think her husband was one. I think it was just because the minister would marry them cheaper than anyone else. I think that's awful. When I get married I'm going to have it done by a minister I believe in, or maybe a priest if I decide to become Catholic.

"Norman wore a dark blue suit and had his hair all combed, and I wore my mom's earrings, you know, the ones that have the little roses on them and a long pink dress to cover up my puffy ankles. All I could think about was all my relatives—on my mom's side, I mean--seeing me with my boyfriend, a nice looking boy even if his teeth weren't all that good. I thought maybe Barbara the psychologist was right. My self-esteem was definitely feeling better.

"But when they were doing all the toasts, Norman said he had to go take a pee, but actually he swiped a bottle of champagne from the bar and went into the bathroom and drank the whole thing. By the time he came back, which was a long time, he was really drunk. I mean really drunk. He was probably drunker than you've ever been in your life, Bob.

"He was so drunk he barfed on the floor, and I had to take him to the bathroom—the girls', because I wouldn't dare go into the boys'—and clean him up. It was really disgusting, and I was really disgusted because I thought I at least I would get one dance out of the first date I had ever been on. But instead I wiped barf off Norman's blue suit with paper towels and water. We had been eating chicken and mixed vegetables, and let me tell you, Bob, I'll never eat chicken and mixed vegetables again. And then my Aunt Judy came in and, boy, was she shocked to see us but had to go into the stall anyway because she had to go that bad.

"Oh, I can't stand that song! I'm going to try for the umpteenth time to get that station that plays the eighties and nineties music. It's so staticky it drives me crazy, but I love the songs they play. I just hope they don't play anything by Sheryl Crowe. It really makes me sad. I just hope doctors can do something for her. What do you think, Bob? I said, what do you think, Bob? About Sheryl Crowe? I guess some people just don't have an opinion about things like that. That's all right with me if they don't.

"But after our quote-unquote date Norman was really different. He wouldn't smile around me or even look me in the eye. When I was sick, I had to ask Becka Donleavy for her notes. It was just all too weird for me. I felt like it was all my fault, only God knows what I had done wrong. Hope you don't mind me saying God, Bob. Hope it's not against the constitution. That's just another joke, I know it's not. Not yet anyway.

"So one day I just said to him, Norman, I said, nobody thinks bad of you because you got drunk and puked at my cousin's wedding. When my dad heard about it, he laughed. He said that just about every teenager does something like that at one time or another, even some grown-ups, and even he did it a few times before he wised up.

"So Norman said, 'So you don't hate me for spoiling your cousin's wedding?' And I said, 'I had a nice time. Except for cleaning up your puke. That was definitely the low point of the afternoon.' And then we both laughed and it was nice to see him smile again. And after that things were back to normal but we never did have another date, of the quote-unquote type or any other.

"Oh, Bob, there's the back of page two that you didn't fill out. That's your medical history, and if I let you skip that the doc would fire me for sure. I know, I hate that pen! If you shake it real well sometimes it helps. The only thing else I have is a big, thick red marker and a pencil, and you can't use a pencil because somebody else could erase one of your answers and fill in something else. Not that anybody here would do that. It's just the principle of the thing.

"So after we graduated, Norman went on to BU. That's Boston University—in Massachusetts. I always say that's in Massachusetts because there's a Boston in Virginia. Or is that South Boston? I'm not sure. I'll have to look that up sometime. It's probably on the Internet, don't you think?

"I used to e-mail him. Norman. The guy I went out with in high school. And he would write me back all about what it was like at college, and I would tell him what was going on back here. He hated his roommate—a guy who listened to show music and told everybody he was gay even though no one knew if he really was or not—but I don't think he had many friends. Norman, I mean. I don't know if the gay guy had friends or not. He may have, but Norman didn't seem to.

"One day he wrote me that he was lonely and missed me. I couldn't believe it. I wanted to tell my psychologist about it, only I couldn't afford it, and I didn't think my mom would pay for me to go back just to do that. But it made me so happy that Norman said he missed me. I wrote him and said that I missed him, too, and that I had a big surprise for him.

"What do think the surprise was? Bet you can't guess, Bob. I said, 'What do you think the surprise was?' The one I had for Norman. Well, I'll tell you. I got a train ticket to Boston and went up to see him without telling him. I was so excited. I was working at Winkie's, and I was supposed to work that weekend, but I left anyway. That's why I lost my job at Winkie's. It only paid $6.50 an hour plus tips that I never got, and this job pays $7.20, and I don't get tips here either. Unless you'd like to tip me, Bob. Twenty dollars would be nice. No, I'm only kidding. I don't expect anyone to tip me in this job.

"Well, I don't know what I was expecting. To be honest, I do know what I was expecting, and I'll tell you. I was expecting a really big reception. I thought he would be so glad to see me he would hug me, and we would go out to dinner, and he would show me around Boston, and then we would go back to his dorm, and his so-called gay roommate would be gone and we would have sex. That's why I brought a condom with me. I brought a condom and a bottle of champagne. Just for a joke. Well, the condom wasn't a joke, just the champagne.

46

"I had never had sex before, and I didn't know if it would hurt. I guess men don't have that problem. I'm sure the first time you had sex, Bob, you weren't worried about it hurting, but I was.

"So anyway, I rang up Norman in his dorm room from the lobby. You can't just go up to a room, you know. It's a regulation. So he comes down to get me, and he looks at me and says, 'How did you get here?' and I said, 'I took the train,' and he says, 'What are you doing in Boston?' and I said, 'Surprise, I came to visit you!' and he says, 'Oh.' That's all he said. Just 'Oh.'

"So I followed him up to his room. His quote-unquote gay roommate was gone for the weekend, and I sat down on his bed—the roommate's, not Norman's—and I gave him the champagne. I was so nervous. I thought that we were going to have sex any minute, but he just put the bottle in his closet and turned the TV on. He told me he wanted to watch the end of this movie. It was about these people who die after watching this really gross movie. I think it was *The Ring* I'm not sure.

"Then we went to eat pizza at a pizza place. I said, 'I missed you back home,' and he said, 'No, you didn't.' I don't know why he said that, do you? It was a weird thing to say. I guess he thought it was weird too, because he seemed embarrassed and didn't say much after that. Then we went to this really crowded bar where you could hardly move, and he said, 'I've got to talk to some people," and after that I didn't know where he was. I went looking for him but I couldn't find him. I think he left the bar with his friends and forgot that I was there.

"I took a taxi back to his dorm. It cost me five dollars! I think that was a rip-off, but I'd never been to Boston before, and I didn't know how to find a bus. So I sat in the lobby until he came back. Well, I started off sitting. Then I lay down on some chairs and fell asleep. Then in the middle of the night Norman came back in. Well, I guess it was really in the middle of the night. I didn't have a watch.

"Okay, thanks, Bob. Are you sure you have everything filled out? I hope you don't mind if I make sure. Okay, that looks good. Yep. Oh, Bob, I see you've had occasional rectal bleeding. That must be awful! I can't imagine having bleeding coming from there. Having my period is bad enough. We had one woman in here who had rectal bleeding, and it turned out she had cancer. I think it was colon cancer. I can't remember if it was or not, and she doesn't come back here anymore. But I wouldn't worry, Bob. Yours is just occasional. That's probably from trying too hard when you go to the bathroom. I've done that before, but I've never had any bleeding.

"So, like I was saying, Norman came back to the dorm—finally! He was pretty drunk. Not as drunk as he was at my cousin's wedding, but pretty drunk. He said, 'You can't sleep there all night,' and I said, 'Well, Norman, I already slept here for half the night.' Like I said, I didn't know if it was half the night or not.

"When we went up to his room he fell down on his bed and passed out. So that was the end of my thinking I was ever going to have sex. I curled up on his roommate's bed—the one that belonged to the quote-unquote gay guy—and I cried and cried. I was so sad. I couldn't understand why he would have been so mean to me. I just knew that if Norman Geckle, the only boy who had ever been nice to me, could treat me like that, then no other person would ever love me, and I'd never have anyone say they loved me. I guess I had lost all my self-esteem, not that I ever had much anyway. I wanted to scream at Barbara the psychologist for ever trying to get me to like myself in the first place, but instead I just cried and cried until I couldn't catch my breath and then I fell asleep. When I got up Norman was still passed out, so I took the bus to the train station. I cried all the way home.

"Well, it shouldn't be too much longer now. I'll just clip this to your chart so the doc can look at it. Oh, here's my favorite song, 'When Sunny Came Home.' Do you like that song? You probably can't hear the words because of the bad reception in here. It's about a girl who burns down her parents' house. That's so mean. I would never do that. I wouldn't even burn down Norman Geckle's house. I can't blame him that he didn't like me. I can really be annoying. I don't know why. I don't want to be. I just am.

"There's that phone again. I hate it when the phone rings, especially when I'm trying to listen to something on the radio. Oh, well, it's part of my job and, besides, if I let the phone just ring and ring, it would really drive me crazy.

"Oh, Bob, the doctor will see you now."

This story was written in the beginning of 2006 while I was in a writers' group including friends Chris Brown and Katrina Denza, who thought some of the characters in the story were based on them. They didn't appreciate it.

Published in Foliate Oak, *Best of 2006 edition, print and online. They published until May 2017.*

god is gay

J oyce greets you at her back door, the one that leads into her
kitchen. Her eyes, the color of a California winter, tell you
she is tired as usual. Her hair is untamed, held back by a band
of paisley cloth—as usual.

The men are already there, sitting at the table under the
light of a copper drop lamp. James wears a white turtleneck,
but first you notice his moustache—thin and gray, betraying
his concern for every detail of his appearance. Patrick, slumped
in the chair across from him, has not shaved.

"Good evening, Theresa," James says to you. Patrick is
drinking from his bottled water. He raises his left hand and
wiggles his fingers in your direction.

You take your place between the two men, laying your file
folder on crumbs left from dinner. You take out the stapled
sheets that are the month's offering from the members of your
writers' support group.

"Who goes first?" asks James.

Joyce brings a glass of iced tea to the table. It smells of mint. "Let's do Theresa's story," she says.

You see the others shuffle through their papers, bringing to the surface the sheet with your name in the upper left corner. You have the luxury of dismissing the fleeting feeling that grips your stomach.

"I love the title," says Joyce.

"What does it mean?" Patrick asks.

Before you have a chance to answer, Joyce says, "It's an explication of the entire story."

"Not an explication," James says. "An explication is an analysis of a literary work. A title can't be an explication. Perhaps you mean elucidation."

"Elucidation?" Patrick puts his water bottle on the floor, a sign that he is ready to offer his opinions. "'god is gay'? What could that possibly elucidate? It has nothing to do with the rest of the story. And why the lower case? Didn't Eliot do that to death?"

"The title has everything to do with the story," Joyce says, nodding at you. "The main character is caught in a conflict between sexual and religious ambiguity. The use of lower case is a rebuttal of patriarchal retribution."

"A statement against capital punishment?" ventures James.

"Just look at the first sentence,' says Joyce. "'You tumble to your knees on the floorboards of your decaying porch, parched and rough-hewn.'"

"Why use the second person present tense?" Patrick asks, not you but Joyce. "I mean, other than to sound trendy?"

"God, Patrick. Sometimes I can't tell if you're being incredibly rude or just plebeian."

"Do you mean presumptuous?" asks James.

"That too," says Joyce. "The second person present tense draws the reader into the story. Can't you see that?"

"Well, why not use the first person plural past imperfect? 'We used to fall to our knees.'"118

Or how about the second person subjunctive? 'May you fall to your knees.' I don't know about you, but that would really draw me into a story."

"Thank you for clarifying it for me, Patrick. Now I know you're just being incredibly rude."

James folds his hands together as if the gesture would be palliative. "I think the use of the present tense distinguishes the flashback from the current action. But one thing does confuse me, Theresa. When you say parched and rough-hewn, are you referring to you or the porch?"

"To me?" you ask.

"Well, to the main character. The you."

"But I'm not the main character," you say. "The main character is a woman who cuts off her fingers."

"Is that what happens?" asks Patrick. "All I could tell was that she was holding a butcher's knife. I thought the bit about giving her ex-husband a hand meant she wanted to help him."

"She does," says Joyce. "That's why she does what she does. To wake him from his hetero-erotic lethargy. But, Theresa, I thought she had cut off her husband's hand."

You smile at the look of hopeful expectation on her thin face. "No, she cuts off her own fingers. The reference to giving a hand means she's applauding him."

"Oh," says Patrick. "That's going to be easy for her with no fingers."

"I like it," says James. "It's quite Zen."

Patrick scratches the stubble on his left cheek. A worn band-aid is wrapped around his middle finger. He doesn't look at you when he speaks. "So what's her motivation for doing something so drastic?"

You stare at him, hoping he'll somehow feel your gaze and finally make eye contact. You tell him it's because she had been sexually molested.

"You mean by the old woman who comes to groom her Chihuahua."

"The amount of detail was remarkable," James says.

"About that," says Joyce. "I was a little disturbed by the graphicness of it. I was reading it aloud to my husband in bed—I hope you don't mind—and when we got to the point where the dog starts…well you know what I mean, Gary ran into the bathroom and threw up."

James says, "You have a dangling participle in the second paragraph on page three." You follow Joyce and Patrick as they turn to the third page. "'Grieving for your lost innocence, Rover offers you a whine of compassion.'"

"I think it's correct," Joyce says. "It's Rover who's grieving. He's symbolic of the latent sexual energy that's been fermenting in her soul."

"I think perhaps you mean fomenting," says James.

"No, fermenting is right," Patrick says. "Theresa just meant a W-I-N-E of compassion. I think a Chihuahua might choose a Rioja Alta '94."

"Go to hell, Patrick." Joyce narrows her eyes. "No one is amused. Either by you or your stories."

Patrick shrugs and reaches for his water, you think, as an infant seeks the security of a bottle. You feel pity for him. He's been writing a story each month for years and has never had one published—not even online. He takes a drink, and a small trickle forms on the corner of his mouth.

"You don't like my story, Patrick?"

"I'm sorry, but I'm just being honest. This woman has no redeeming characteristics whatsoever. I despise her from the get-go. I don't care what she does to herself or whatever the hell seems to happen to her."

"Some of it is a little challenging to follow," says James.

"Just a little," says Joyce.

"And your figures of speech," Patrick says. "The corn holders lie in the drawer like wrinkled Chinamen in a trundle bed. The corn holders don't have anything to do with the story." He points a sudden finger toward Joyce. "And don't give me any bullshit about the symbolic meaning of the corn holders, either."

"I think it was Freud," says James, "who said that sometimes a corn holder is simply a corn holder."

"Admit it, Theresa," Patrick says finally looking at you. "You're just showing off your ability to come up with colorful figures of speech. They don't do a thing to advance the narrative."

"Why does everything have to advance the narrative?" asks Joyce. "You simply have no understanding of experimental literature, Patrick. This isn't a narrative story."

"You're telling me," he says.

"It does have an almost poetic structure, Theresa," says James. "I found the ending to have a classical allusion. A modern *deus ex machina*."

"A blind Norwegian parachuter gets blown off course and lands in her front yard?" Patrick looks again to you, his eyes the color of a Tidy-bowl toilet. "Or did I get it wrong?"

"I didn't say he was Norwegian," you tell him. "I just said he was Scandinavian."

"Well that clears things up," he says. "I had trouble buying a Norwegian ending up on a desolate farm in Montana. But a Scandinavian! That's different."

"Fuck you, Patrick. Who needs you in our group, anyway?"

"Oh, come on, Joyce. Can you tell me honestly that you enjoyed a thoroughly depressing story about a deeply disturbed woman who lives an agonizing life in a decrepit house?"

"It's naturalism, Patrick. It's life. It's part of the human experience we all share."

"What do you mean 'we?' Theresa is a Vassar graduate with

two children, an SUV, and a husband who's a stockbroker."

"I have to agree with Patrick that the piece is a bit dark," says James.

"Maybe you could leave out the part where she finds the head of the rabbi in the microwave," Joyce says.

"I'm afraid it's too late," you tell them. "You see I've already sent it off."

An awkward pause circles the table. You have broken one of the unspoken rules of the group—submitting a story before it's been critiqued.

"Oh," says Joyce. "Well, I suppose that's that. I know we all wish you luck."

"It's too late even for that," you say, stifling a smile you know will seem smug. "It's already been accepted by *The American Pedantic Literary Review*."

"Congratulations," says Joyce.

"I knew this was an excellent piece," says James.

Patrick reaches for his bottle.

Olives and Prunes

In less than a minute Joel will do something he never thought himself capable of doing. It won't be courage that compels him. It won't be the result of calculated risk. It will be done without thinking, the consequence of thinking too much.

He sits on the worn red seat of the local train that runs from the city to his stop in the suburbs. The train is now beginning to slow for his stop. It's on time, 2:35 p.m. He took the train home after pleading he was too sick to finish the day at work. He really was sick; it wasn't simply an excuse to leave a job he despised. He was going home to his empty apartment where he would lie in his bed, wishing there were someone to wipe his forehead if he vomited.

The Local would be overflowing in a couple of hours, but now it was quiet. He had never been on the train when it was that quiet. A woman had gotten on the same car and sat down directly across from him. She was extraordinarily pretty, somewhere in her thirties, Joel guessed. She had smooth cheekbones that looked is if they would smile along with her mouth. But she wasn't smiling. She was staring at the floor although there was nothing to warrant her attention. Her eyes were dark—engaging but melancholy.

Her sweater was a violet crew neck, maybe cashmere. It was long enough to cover her lap and spill over her dark slacks. He couldn't tell what her figure might be; the sweater was too loose. She wore a dark blue scarf that hid her hair. A woman that attractive must have beautiful hair. Maybe she was a blonde.

Joel tried not to think about the weakness and nausea that came in unpredictable waves. He thought instead about the woman and decided she looked like her name might be Elizabeth. He guessed she was coming home from town after a lunch date with a friend, someone she had known since college. Her friend's name, he decided, was Rebecca.

They had eaten at Bertucci's. Elizabeth arrived after her friend was seated and was waving at her from a booth near the window.

"I'm sorry to be late," Elizabeth said, catching her breath. "I hurried…"

"Of course you did," said Rebecca. "It's nothing at all. I've just gotten here." Rebecca had short hair that fell across her forehead—carefully styled to seem casual—and black, much darker than Nature had provided. She used makeup to court male attention.

"Would you care for a drink?" The young waiter was glad to have customers at his table that late in the lunch hour.

"Just bottled water," Elizabeth said.

"Not a martini?" Rebecca asked, sipping her own.

"I'm off alcohol. I'm sorry," as if an apology were needed. The waiter left, mentally subtracting the difference between 20% of a water and that of a mixed drink.

"How are you, dear?"

Elizabeth despised that question, especially when it ended with a patronizing endearment. "Well..." Her hand instinctively went to straighten her hair before she remembered she was wearing a scarf. "Fine today, thanks. How about you?"

"Oh, me? You know I'm always the same. But I came here to talk about you. Are you still seeing Dr. Hunt?"

"Yes."

"I've heard the man's a scoundrel. He's been having an affair for years with a woman who used to be a patient of his. Doesn't that just make your skin crawl, thinking about him examining her, then having the gall to have a sexual relationship? But no one will take away his license for something like that. Consensual, I suppose."

"I suppose."

The waiter materialized with the bottled water. "Are you ladies ready to order?" He asked the question of Rebecca whose black lace blouse had caught his eye when she sat down.

"Oh, Jesus. Elizabeth, you look through the menu while I order. I know what I want." She smiled at the waiter. "I'll have the spiced stuffed olive salad, but leave off the lettuce. I just want the olives."

"Just the olives," he repeated, showing neither disappointment nor disapproval.

"I'm simply crazy for spiced olives, and Bertucci's has the best in the city. Did you know that…"

Joel could picture the waiter. Early twenties. Superficially pleasant face. Short hair and a discreet earring. When he seated her he had introduced himself as Paul.

"…did you know that, Paul?"

"I'll be sure to tell the chef." He smiled knowing he wouldn't. "And for you, ma'am?" he asked Elizabeth who, although he thought her undeniably attractive, wore a distinctly unstylish scarf. He was holding out hope she would order one of the specials, several of which they still had in the kitchen.

"Oh, do have the olives, too," Rebecca said.

Elizabeth squirmed slightly in the booth. The thought of olives was unbearable. "No, she said. "I don't think so. I think I'll just have some fruit. Do you have anything fresh?"

"I'll check," he said, feigning politeness.

"No, wait. Do you have prunes? Maybe a little cottage cheese and some prunes."

Paul took the menus from the table as if they had been a waste of time. "Sure," he said. "Stuffed olive salad, no lettuce, and prunes with cottage cheese." And then he vanished.

"Prunes?" Rebecca asked.

There was so much that was awkward to explain. "The radiation hasn't been very kind," Elizabeth said. "Prunes help."

Rebecca took Elizabeth's hands. "You poor dear. I want to hear everything. Do you hear from Ian?"

Ian is Elizabeth's husband. Her ex, Joel decided. They had been separated just before she had been diagnosed.

"He's moving to Baltimore."

"Not Baltimore? Do you know Jack…oh, what's his last name? Maguire—something like Maguire—I'll be forgetting my own name next. He's what's-her-name's husband. He's from Baltimore. He says the city is a dump. I've only been through it on I-95. Never wanted to stop there, though. McKenzie, that's what it is. Jack McKenzie, Carolyn's husband. How could I forget? Do you think that's normal for a woman of our age to be so forgetful?"

"I don't know. I suppose so."

"So tell me what you've been doing with yourself. Are you still working? Of course you're not. You wouldn't be here if you were still working. I've been thinking about getting a job. I really have. But I help out with lunch at Brian's school on Thursdays. I'd hate to stop that. It means so much to him. Did I show you his soccer picture?" Rebecca put her black purse on the table and opened the clasp. "He's turning into the cutest little athlete." She brought out an Italian leather wallet that opened from a gold clasp. "Here."

The boy was blonde and smug, standing with one leg on a ball. Elizabeth was barely seeing him. "He's very handsome," she said.

"You know I always hoped you and Ian would have a child. You're both such attractive people. But I guess that's not going to happen."

Elizabeth's throat tightened despite her efforts. She tried to remember what it was like when she was the lead in her high school senior spring play. She trained herself to cry on command. She hoped she could trade those tears for the ones she felt gaining pressure behind her eyes.

"I suppose not," she said.

"Oh, my dear Lizzie. I didn't mean to upset you."

The rush overwhelmed Elizabeth's façade, and the pain of embarrassment seemed preferable to the pain of remaining. "You'll have to excuse me, Rebecca. I'm suddenly not feeling well." She slid from the booth and stood.

"You're not leaving? Oh, Lizzie, you can't make me eat alone?"

Joel can't bear the awkwardness of the situation he's creating. The waiter, he thinks, must reappear with their food.

"Maybe Paul could sit with you," Elizabeth said. "There's hardly anyone else in here now. Would you, Paul? Just for a few moments? This is Rebecca."

"Hello, Rebecca." He smiled.

"Olives and prunes?" Rebecca said, now looking at the plates in the waiter's hands."

"I'm terribly sorry. I'll call you," Elizabeth had said, leaving.

Now the train has stopped at Rosemont Station. The woman is standing at the door, waiting for it to open. Joel rises and stands behind her even though his car is parked three stops away. He follows her onto the platform. He's slightly dizzy. He can't remember ever speaking to a stranger without a reason, certainly never a beautiful woman.

"Excuse me," he says, touching her on the shoulder of her loose violet sweater. He steps forward, parallel to her. She had never looked at him on the train, but now she sees him.

"There are a lot of selfish, self-centered people in the world," he says.

She says nothing.

"But there are also people who are compassionate and kind."

She says, "I suppose so." Her face—the beautiful face beneath the mysterious blue scarf. His stomach lurches involuntarily.

The edges of his vision dim and he finds himself behind the station house, on his knees vomiting. When he finishes heaving without result, he becomes aware that someone is standing behind him.

"Are you all right?" A long strand of saliva hangs from his mouth. He feels weak but restored enough to be violently embarrassed.

"Yes," he says to her. "I think I must have a stomach flu."

"Is there anything I can do for you?"

"No, thank you. I'll be all right."

"Are you sure?"

He stands, still consumed with shame. He wants to buy her a cup of coffee and listen to her unburden herself of the melancholy in her eyes, but thinks of Pygmalion.

"I'm fine, really."

She looks doubtful but walks down to the parking lot.

The year after I published The Woman in the Wilderness *in 2005, Amazon introduced a program called Amazon Shorts. They accepted short stories for online publication which they sold for $1 per read. This was still years before ebooks were introduced. I was doing what I could to promote* The Woman, *so I wrote this story as if it were sort of a missing chapter from the book, and it was accepted in December 2006. I believe the Amazon Shorts program is still active without the same name, as a program selling short stories to Kindle readers in ebook format.*

The Wizard of The Wissahickon

June 24, 1700
Germantown, Province of Pennsylvania
North America

T here was a tangible current of anticipation that flowed from the air, through the hand of his mother and into Josiah's chest. Rain waited in the sky, the milder of two expectations. Beyond the sky was the more anxious promise, an encounter with the curious mystic, the *Einsiedler* of the Wissahickon, who was waiting for them in his tabernacle in the wilderness beyond the village of the Germans.

"Grüß Gott!" It was yet another German, another of the non-English people whom William Penn had invited to share his utopian dream. Josiah's mother had told him that The Proprietor was part German and partial to those whose religion marked them as outcasts at best. The few Germans

living in Philadelphia were not Quakers or even Anglicans. They subscribed to odd religions, spoke in a strange guttural language, and held a continual reserve. Here in Germantown, in the heart of their own settlement, they were everywhere.

"Are you the dear Sister Hannah?" The tall man, struggling in thick English, asked Josiah's mother. He was dressed in a woolen robe like a picture from an illustrated Bible, but his clean-shaven upper lip and bushy beard marked him, not as a prophet, but as a religious non-conformist. "And that thy child be?" He knelt down, eye level with Josiah's sister. "*Grüß Gott, liebes Fräulein* Maria."

"Mary," corrected Josiah's mother.

Mary was not right. Josiah had known at her birth, her eyes strangely angled, and the persistent jerky movements of her infancy followed her into childhood. Josiah's mother bore the burden alone as his father was still away "at sea." Those two words had been repeated so often Josiah now believed them to be a deceit. By age eleven he was painfully aware of his mother's trial—a lonely struggle that had dragged her through whispered tales of a strange and powerful healer, led her along the Great Road to Germantown, and now was beckoning her toward the wild forests of the Wissahickon Valley.

"Seelig called am I," said the German in the robe, rising. "Answering your letter was me. Now, to please take you to *der Magister* may I?" He offered his arms to carry Mary, but the girl fell to the security of her mother's leg.

"No, no, no!"

He bent to her level again. Mary tightened her grip and pulled away from the stranger. Seelig brought a long-fingered hand from the loose sleeve of his robe and took the child's chin.

He stared into her eyes. Josiah, unsure of the intent, tensed as he always did when he sensed his sister's vulnerability.

Suddenly the German stood, turned, and started down the street, away from the mule cart which had brought the family the six miles from Philadelphia. "Come, please. Haste make us."

Hannah took Mary in her arms, kissed her and set her down on the cobblestones. "We are going on a walk, Mary. There is a man who lives in the woods who wants to help us."

That was the explanation she had given the children. For a week after she had read the letter, her usual despondency had been infiltrated with an optimism that frightened Josiah. She hadn't scolded him for his negligence delivering the laundry they took in, nor for his inattentiveness to his studies. The healer, who had not been identified more than with the single name *Kelpius*, had upset the familiar balance of their home with his vague promise. Josiah despised the pity the neighbors inflicted on them, but he had come to accept Mary's condition in a way his mother was unable to do. His most anxious worry was that this uncharacteristic atmosphere of hope would lead to a crushing disappointment. He loved his mother with a fervor he unconsciously believed would make up for the love she lacked from anyone else.

Seelig's hand came down on Josiah's shoulder. "Let us hasten, dear friends, " the German said.

Josiah looked up into the man's eyes, hoping for some indication of what lay ahead. He didn't expect to find the intensity in Seelig's gaze, as if the German were searching him as well. It was an unfamiliar feeling, a disturbing feeling, and he turned his gaze to his feet, surprised to find he was already walking. He declined the offer of the German's hand and instead took his mother's, not as her child, but as her protector.

Seelig led the three of them off the cobblestones of the Great Road, beside a field of youthful flax, past the boundary that separated the cleared German land from the virgin forest. As the sky had promised, it began to rain. It started as a light drumming on the leaves, barely noticed beyond its sound until the tops of the giant trees leaked water.

"Momma, Momma. I am wet." Hannah stopped and looked through her carrying bag until she found a white scarf. She bent and tied it around Mary's bonnet. "Carry me, Mother. Carry me."

"Thou art a big girl. It is not much further."

"Carry me, Mother."

The German, who had raised his hood over his head, turned, and made a gesture of help. His face was draped in shadow, wraithlike.

"No, no, no!"

Josiah could hear the urgency in his sister's voice. He stopped. "I will carry thee, Mary."

"Mary will walk," his mother said.

Mary did walk.

The forest was gray with the traces of rain that filtered into the understory. The path took them past clusters of primeval boulders, winding down toward the bottom of the gorge where the creek ran. Josiah knew what was alive in the forests beyond Philadelphia—great horned buck deer, wildcats, bears. The German did not have a gun.

It was more than a half hour down into the gorge. Sometimes the rain spilled from the trees, sometimes retreating into only a threat. The German's long legs constantly carried him ahead of the family until he had to stop and wait. Josiah watched Mary growing more impatient. He kept studying his mother, searching for reassurance that they were going to be safe.

"Is it much further?" Hannah asked. "Mary is not used to walking this far."

Seelig smiled, perhaps reluctant to answer or, Josiah wondered, unable to understand a simple English sentence.

An incline in the path had been covered with small rocks to keep it from washing away. Mary bent down and put her hands into the colorful pebbles.

"Mary, come now."

"No, Momma, no!"

"Yes, this very minute."

Mary's face collapsed into tears.

Seelig lifted the hood from his head and approached the girl. "Wanting to see you now is someone, *liebes Fräulein Maria*," he said.

The German's voice was without a trace of annoyance, as if he were used to speaking to small children. But Josiah did not like the words—the idea that someone was at that moment lying in wait for them in the wet depths of this unending forest.

It was not like him to feel afraid.

"Kelpius, the Wizard of the Wissahickon?" the baker had asked, his eyes wide. "He is an alchemist and liable to keep thee with him as his *familiar*. He has the evil eye. Tell thy mother not to let thee out of her sight."

"They raise the devil there," The farrier whispered as they were leaving the city. The old man smiled, toothless. "When the moon is full they cut out the heart of a virgin to make their potions. Tonight the moon is nearly full."

What if it were true? What if it were a sorcerer his mother was taking them to see and not a healer? If The Hermit were so beneficent, Josiah wondered, why would he be forced to live like an outcast?

Josiah's hat was wet by the time he could first see the water, and fully soaked by the time they reached the precipitous bank. There was no sign of a healer or of a wizard. There was only a bridge of logs, supported by pillars of stone rising from the swirling waters. On the other bank the trail continued.

There was no railing. Josiah took his sister's hand and he helped her walk across. They were six feet or more above the water and he didn't know how to swim.

If the trail to that point had been difficult for Mary, the other side was nearly impossible. The path forced them up the steep side of the gorge and along the edge of a ridge. Josiah could no longer bear the sight of his sister's struggle. He lifted her and she fell against him, her legs tight around his abdomen. She laid her head on his chest.

Josiah could see it finally through the rain, a building claiming the highest point on the ridge. It had been constructed of cedar logs, but it was no cabin. It was massive in girth, more than two stories with a tall lookout protruding above the shake roof. On the summit—not a cross like the one on the Anglican Church—but a circle divided into quarters. A magician's symbol surely. Josiah pulled his sister tighter against him.

Closer, first faintly beneath the drumming of the rain, he could hear voices and the sounds of an organ. "Yay-zoo Kristus." The German name for Jesus. In spite of the odd cross symbol, he thought, it must be some kind of church. He had never been in a church—his Quaker mother had made sure of that—but he knew what one was. Church may have been religious pretension but it wasn't sorcery. He let out a breath into the drizzle and cursed himself for letting the baker and the farrier frighten him.

The path led them into a clearing and an iron entrance in a wooden fence surrounding the church. Seelig opened the gate and followed them along a stone path. There were no stained-glass windows like the ones in Christ Church near their home. There were windows in the building, though, through which the flickering light of candles shone into the summer evening. The rain had stopped and Josiah could hear singing: O yay-zoo lay-re-mich-vee-ich-dich-finde." No one would think to sing at a Quaker meeting.

Josiah let Mary drop from her perch on his hip. She ran to her mother, her thumb in her mouth. He knew she was tired. At home, his sister already would be in bed asleep.

Seelig opened the heavy door. His mother went inside, Mary once again clasping her leg. Josiah had no choice. He followed.

Even the candles and the diffuse light from the windows weren't able to illuminate a room of that size. Josiah had never seen such a room. Its size dwarfed the dozen or so men and women who sat on the floor, singing. Opposite the door a symbol of iron hung from the wall. It was wider than he was tall. A cross within a circle.

"He is a wizard and no Christian," the baker had said.

A small organ stood against a bare wall, at which sat a boy. No, Josiah realized, a frail young man. Josiah could see that his face was without a trace of beard. There was nothing of a sorcerer in his appearance. He bore the unfortunate look of one who had been teased as a child for the sin of a meager stature.

The man did not look at them. He was intent on leading the hymn.

"Herr Kelpius," Seelig whispered, nodding his head, *"der Magister."*

Josiah didn't know what that word meant. He assumed it was German for priest and not for wizard. He wondered if his mother had known this is what they were going to find at the end of their long journey from Philadelphia—an oversized German church in the woods.

He took off his hat in imitation of the other men in the room and ran his fingers through his wet hair. He looked at his mother. The rain had soaked her bonnet as well. She betrayed no emotion, just focused attention toward the man at the organ. Was she as disappointed as he? He could not bear more of her tears.

The singing stopped and the young priest stood to speak. "Ach-gib-uns-noya hertzen." Why, Josiah thought, don't these people learn to speak English? After all, Pennsylvania was an English province, given to an Englishman by the English King.

Mary pointed toward the young man. "Momma, who is that?" she asked in a voice that overtook the soft tones of the priest. Two dozen German eyes turned toward them. Whenever people stared at Mary, Josiah burned with humiliation. "Mama, take me home. Take me home," the girl said, her voice rising. The priest stopped speaking.

"I present Sister Hanna Pressman, her daughter Maria—Mary—and her son." Herr Seelig looked at Josiah. "How are you called, little *brudder*?"

Josiah flushed. He hated this German for thrusting him into the center of attention. My name is no business of yours, he wanted to scream. "Josiah Pressman," he said instead. "But I am not a brother to you."

There was a ripple of soft laughter.

"Wir sind hier alle Brüder und Schwestern. We are here all brothers and sisters," Herr Seelig said, translating for his unwelcome benefit.

There was a smell of sweet wood burning in the air that turned Josiah's stomach. He tugged at his mother's sleeve in hope he could steal her attention. "Mother, I will wait for thee outside this church."

She turned toward him. "Son, please wait…" Mary began to cry.

Josiah let himself out the heavy door.

The gray rain had given way to a green light rich with moisture. Without the patter on the leaves, without the German choir, the world was full of the sounds of life in the forest. A herb garden on the border of a path to the fence lofted a thick fragrance into the air. Despite the reprimand he was sure to receive from his mother, Josiah was glad he had left. Quakers had no business being in a church, especially a German one.

He knew there would be no healing for Mary. This vain journey was something his father would never have been foolish enough to undertake. But then again, his father had never even seen Mary. He had left while Josiah's mother was still with child. Ever since Josiah was old enough to understand, he wondered if his father were really Mary's father. Maybe, he thought, his cheeks red with shame, that was why his father had never returned.

He would give the baker and the farrier a piece of his mind for frightening him. No, why not repay them in kind? He would tell them that the mysterious *Einsiedler* of the Wissahickon had tried to put on spell on them, but it would not work because of the strength of Josiah's spirit. He would describe in detail a Temple of Sorcery with horrifying beasts—bears with heads of lions—no, men with heads of bears, doomed victims of evil magic. That they barely escaped after he overpowered the old wizard.

But there was no trace of magic in the garden. It was larger than most in town, but not that much different. These were probably German herbs, he supposed. Germans had their own sort of food.

Beyond the garden, on the other side of the fence, was a meadow, and he searched the sky above it for any sign the clouds were breaking. The midsummer evening seemed as if it would last indefinitely, but he and his family had a long way to return home.

He decided he would go behind the building to see what might be there. It was shadowed and unwelcoming. The edge of the ridge was closer there and the forest louder with birds and frogs and—what else? He wished he had not conjured a picture in his mind of men with heads of bears. The vine of a sticker plant grabbed him by the trousers.

"Samuel Pressman."

His heart leapt at his father's name. It was a stranger's voice and, turning toward it, he saw a slight figure coming toward him from around the edge of the building. It was Kelpius, the Magister, the priest.

"Samuel Pressman, where art thou?" the *Einsiedler* came toward him, his right leg dragging slightly. He was dressed in a plain wool robe, hoodless, a wound black cap on his head. There was something wrong with his face. His eye, the same left eye that distorted Mary's face, was half-closed beneath a heavy lid. An evil eye. The warning of the baker flooded back into Josiah's mind.

Josiah stared, unwilling to feel he was afraid, and unable not to.

"Samuel Pressman."

Why was he calling him that?

Kelpius approached him, close enough for the pungent smell of the tabernacle that lingered in his robe to overcome the evening air. He reached out, and put his hand on Josiah's cheek. The *Einsiedler* brought both fearful eyes close to his face, looking not at Josiah, but focused somewhere beyond.

"Why hast thou not returned to thy family?"

Josiah stepped backward, but the *Einsiedler's* hand stayed on his cheek.

"What art thou doing in London?"

"I—am—in Philadelphia. In Germantown." Josiah could hear the thinness of his own voice. He struggled to take command, to waken this German from his trance, to push him away. Josiah was the male head of his family. He would be strong as he had been for so many years.

"Samuel Pressman?"

"My—name—is—Josiah."

"Thou art in Newgate prison, serving a sentence for a crime you did not commit."

A tightness rose in Josiah's throat. "No! I am not."

"You have suffered, unable to write to thy family."

In spite of his heroic resolve, tears came to Josiah's eyes and wouldn't be controlled. They flooded his vision and wet his face. "Do not speak any more," he whispered.

Kelpius closed his eyes. "What are you saying, Samuel Pressman? That you love your son? That you will return to him when you are finally released?"

Take your hand from my face, Josiah thought. He framed the words, but his voice refused to be mustered.

Was it German? Josiah could not understand. The *Einsiedler* was mumbling. "*Fuerchte dich nicht.* Frighten yourself not, Samuel Pressman. Your son is well."

For the briefest moment the *Einsiedler* was no longer in front of him; the forest became stone. Josiah felt the image of a prison cell force itself into his mind. A man lay on a board, not dead but lost in sleep.

Something else was there. A tall form loomed in front of them. Seelig put his hands on Kelpius' shoulder. "I beg a thousand pardons, Josiah Pressman. The Magister does not mean thee any harm. His years in contemplation have caused him subject to spells. "*Kum, Brüder Kelpius, lass uns tsoor gotteshaus zurueckkeyren.*" Let us return to the Tabernacle."

A crowd of the church members stood by the corner of the building, gaping. Josiah's mother held Mary in her arms.

"Perhaps, Josiah," Seelig said with his long arm around the *Einsiedler*, "when the Magister is feeling better, your family may return, and he will be able to bless your sister."

Josiah did not follow. He stood at the edge of the dark, wet forest waiting for his tears to end.

Author's note: *Johannes Kelpius was a Transylvanian-born mystic who lived with a community of brethren on a ridge above the Wissahickon Valley in Pennsylvania between 1694 and 1708. He was known in oral history as a healer, religious philosopher, musician, poet, astronomer, alchemist, and wizard.*

This piece of flash fiction, written in the summer of 2007, was inspired by wondering how culture-bound our stereotypical life changes might be. It is previously unpublished.

Crisis at Nemtehotek

I'm lying here on my pallet, wide awake as usual, wondering when all this began to invade my life. Looking back, I'd have to say that it came upon me so gradually I didn't realize what was happening until it was too late. Yet, I can clearly remember what I used to be like. I used to be happy.

The turning point was the day I was whipped. Not for the first time of course but certainly for the last. My team had moved our stone a half of a parsec, about usual for us. The trouble was, the overseer had brought in a cracker-jack team of young bucks from Akhamemnon. They rolled their stone nearly a full parsec. The overseer took it as a credit to himself, another opportunity to suck up to management. I, being our team leader, was made the scapegoat. With the role came fifty lashes.

Soon afterwards I found myself wondering if that was all there was to life. Through years of hard work, I had earned the position of team leader. Once I believed that someday I might make overseer. What a pathetically naïve dream! The cold truth was that I would grow old and eventually die on the job. I knew there was a mob of youngsters waiting for me to get out of the way so they could take my place. I could smell their ambition.

That spring during the Festival of the Flood, I went for my annual visit to my wife. We still had sex even though she was past the age to bear children. That year it just wasn't the same. She looked bored and even yawned.

When I returned to Nemtehotek there seemed to be something missing, as if I had lost a part of myself. I would get up in the morning and not be able to decide what to wear—the old loincloth or the new one. It didn't seem to matter.

I've always had an eye for chariots. Whenever one would come by, I would watch it out of the corner of my eye. I learned to tell the difference among the different models. There are ordinary sedans, sport-utility models that seat up to six, and luxury models with leather interiors and four-on-the-floor horses. At night, I would dream I owned a chariot that I could race around for the mere fun of it.

So I've made my decision. Before dawn I'm going to break my shackles with a stone I've been hiding. I've never seen the big river to the east, but I know it's there. When I reach it, I'll build a raft of tree branches and reeds and float right out of the Kingdom. I'll find a land where they are interested in more than just building pyramids in the desert. I'll teach the inhabitants how to build chariots. They'll make me a leader, and I'll have my own fleet. I'll be able to ride wherever I please.

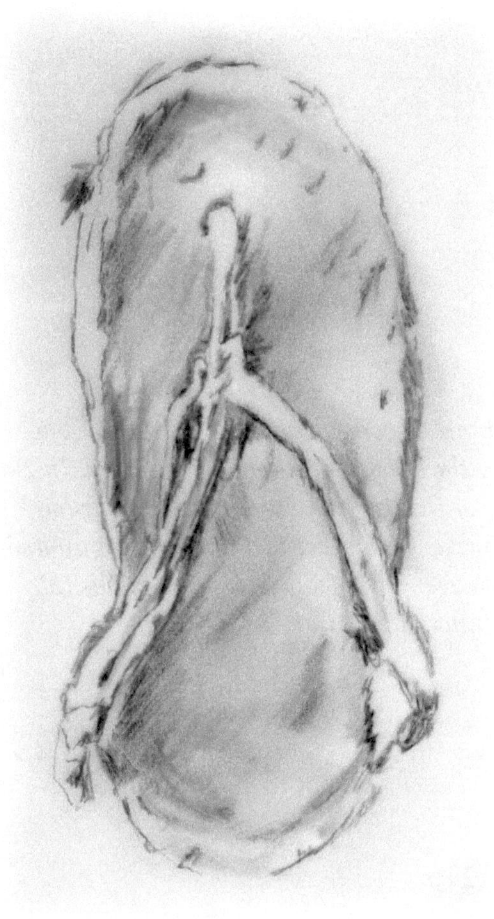

*"The Root of Evil" is very much a product of its time, written during the administration of G.W. Bush. In 2007, it won a prize for fiction in the now-defunct journal, **Shallah**. The prize was the contact email for an up-and-coming literary agent. This story was also published in the now-defunct* 4nada *in February 2008.*

The Root of Evil

"When did you submit your claim?"

"More than a week."

"Your name?"

"Wilson. James Wilson."

"What exactly was the nature of your world's record, Mr. Wilson?"

"It weren't a world's record, per se. It was what you call an oddity. It was a potato that looked like Osama bin Laden."

I could hear a painful sound through the phone receiver. "Yes, I do remember that. You see, Mr. Wilson, what we're looking for are world's records."

"But you got a man in 1936 who grew a turnip what looked like Franklin Roosevelt."

"Well, that was different. Roosevelt was a national hero. Osama bin Laden is a despised terrorist. Besides, we can't take a photograph as evidence, they're so easily retouched these days. Do you still have the potato?"

"Yeah, it's in the freezer, but it's getting old and froze."

"Too bad, Mr. Wilson. Now if you had eaten the most number of potatoes in one minute…"

* * *

"Come in and sit down, James."

"Thank you, Reverend. Sure is nice of you to take the time."

"Always have time for a parishioner. Although I can't say I've seen much of you in church. How's Maudine?"

"I'd be lying if I said she was fine, Reverend. Money being the way it is."

"Take all things to the Lord in prayer, James."

"Well, that's just it, sir. That's how this all started."

He took off his glasses and rubbed his eyes. "Is this about your potato?"

"Yes, sir. You see, just about the time my unemployment run out, Maudine got fired from Ms. Gilmore's and, on top of that, our apartment building's bein' tore down. Jimmy broke his arm playing basketball and we had to take him to the emergency room. Seven hundred twenty-seven dollars and thirty-five cents."

"I'm sorry to hear that. But if you…"

"Maudine just broke down, Reverend. She wore herself sick that we'd wind up on the streets. She's heard you tell take all things to the Lord in prayer, and so she decided to do just that. She took it all to the Lord in prayer. She first did it in the quiet of her heart, you know, but soon she was shouting 'Jesus, Jesus' so loud that they started banging on the ceiling."

"It started getting on my nerves, not that I mind hearing

the name of the Lord, Reverend. But finally I went outside to take out the garbage and this potato rolled out of the bag."

"The potato that looked like Osama bin Laden?"

"The very same one. It had to be the answer to our prayers. It just had to be. I mean, how many times in a man's life does he find a potato with a face on it? And somebody that famous. I mean, it had his turban and everything."

The man started cleaning his fingernails. "Yes, James. I heard about it. But why is this something you've come to me about?"

"Here's the thing, sir. God performed this miracle, and a real miracle it was, but it don't seem to have brought any cash with it."

"Well, James, the Lord moves in mischievous ways, His wonders to perform."

"I thought it was 'mysterious ways,' Reverend."

"Whatever," he said.

*   *   *

"James, there's a white man on the phone. He says he's from the TV."

I had to get up off the can to answer the phone.

"Good evening, Mr. Wilson. My name is Lorenzo McTavish. I'm with WPVI, channel 53."

"We don't get cable," I told him.

"What's he want?" Maudine shouted to me from the kitchen.

"We're a local community access station. I heard about you and your potato from Mrs. Monroe from your church.

Her nephew works with my sister at the glass works. I'd like to bring out a camera crew to your home and interview you."

"You want to come here?"

"Lord! Don't let nobody from the TV come into this apartment!" Maudine said. "What's he want to come here for, anyway?"

I held my hand over the receiver. "He wants to interview me."

"About the potato?"

"Yeah, the potato."

"Praise Jesus! How much is he gonna pay you?"

I took my hand off the receiver. "How much does this pay?"

He snickered. "Oh, we can't pay you, Mr. Wilson. We're only allowed to pay you if you're a member of the Screen Actors' Guild. Are you a member of the Screen Actors' Guild?"

"How much?" Maudine asked.

"No, sir. I'm sure not a member of that," I said.

"The thing is, Mr. Wilson, today fame is money. We had a man on our show once who invented a machine for removing ear wax and he got a hundred thousand dollars from a venture capital firm."

"Lord! Do you think I could get that much?"

"How much?" Maudine asked again.

"A hundred thousand dollars from adventure capital."

"Hallelujah! Thank you, Lord. Thank you, Lord!" Maudine came into the living room and fell down on her knees.

"Now the thing is, Mr. Wilson, I can't promise that anything like that will happen to you."

"No, sir."

"I mean, finding a potato with the face of Osama bin Laden isn't like inventing an ear wax machine."

"No, sir."

"But you never can tell."

I can always tell when a white man is talking down to me. "Just what is your show, Mr. McTavish?"

"It's an investigative reporting show, sort of like 60 Minutes. It's called "Wonders, Weirdos, and Wackos."

"You can quit your praising, Maudine."

*   *   *

"Are you nervous, Mr. Wilson?"

"No, sir. I mean, I suppose a little, sir."

"Well, there's no need. My viewers just want to see you as you are."

"Oh, no. We don't want nobody to see us as we are. Maudine's been driving herself crazy fixing things up. The stress just knocked her off her regularity."

I thought a little joke might lighten things up. I was right. He started laughing.

"That's great, Jim. May I call you Jim? That's just the sort of thing I'd like you to say on camera. Mike, let's get this thing rolling. This guy's a pistol."

A little red light came on the front of the camera. I could feel beads of sweat start on my forehead

"I'd like you to meet Jim Wilson, the man who claims he found a potato with an amazing shape. Is that right, Jim?"

"Sure is. Only it wasn't so much the shape as it was the wrinkles and the spots."

"Now here we have a picture that Jim says he took of the potato. Can you zoom in on it, Mike? Over here. No, that's about as steady as I can hold it. Now, you say you think this looks like…who? Would you tell us?"

"Osama bin Laden. You should know that already, Mr. McTavish, I've already told you. Look here, don't mind my fingers. You see, these lines are his turban and those two spots are his eyes and that little crack is his mouth right above his beard."

"Hmmm. What do you think, folks? A potato with the face of Osama bin Laden? Or is it just a clever ruse? Do you own a copy of Photoshop, Jim?"

"No, sir. I sure don't. I'm not sure what that is."

"It's retouching software for the computer."

This man was getting on my nerves. "I don't own a computer."

"That so?" He looked into the camera and made a face with his eyebrows. "Do you still have the potato?"

I had it in the pocket of my nice blue jacket. "Here it is, Mr. McTavish. It's been in the freezer for a couple of weeks. Looking back, I don't think that was the best thing to do. It's sort of turned ill on me."

"Well, I'd say he doesn't look at his best." He held it up.

"Wrong side, Mr. McTavish. Here, let me turn it around."

"Ah yes. Looks a little like Mr. bin Laden had a big night out on the town. And speaking of that, have you ever had any contact with al-Queda, Jim?"

"Huh? What? No! I'm a loyal American and a veteran."

"Right. Were you ever stationed overseas?"

"Yeah, but what…?"

"In the Middle East?"

"I served in Desert Storm if that's what…"

"Were you ever in Saudi Arabia, Jim?"

"No! Not me, I mean, not just me. My unit was there. But it was just six weeks."

He did that thing with his eyebrows. "So, Jim, is there some connection between you and bin Laden?"

"There ain't a connection except I almost bit his head off in my potato salad. I think I've had enough." I stood up.

"Just a couple more questions about where you were on September 11, 2001. What are you doing? Hey, easy! That's an expensive shirt! Better cut the camera, Mike."

* * *

"Good God! Didn't we pull the cord on the phone?"

"It's not the phone this time, James. It's the doorbell."

"The doorbell? Let me see what time is it. Three-twenty in the morning!"

"Better go answer it."

"Well, I'll answer it enough to knock the block off anybody who comes and rings my doorbell at three-twenty in the morning."

I pulled some pants on over my shorts while I hopped into the living room. "Hold your horses." I said so whoever it was could hear me.

It was two white men wearing suits. "What the hell do you want?" I asked, not feeling very polite. The day before I had had four phone calls and Maudine three.

"James Wilson?"

"If I ain't, I got the wrong driver's license."

They stepped in. "I'm agent Reaves and this is agent Murdoch. We're from the National Security Agency." He flashed something at me. For all I knew—it was three-twenty in the morning—it could have been something he got from a cracker jack box.

"Who is it, James?"

"Couldn't this wait until morning?" I asked.

"Where the security of the nation is concerned, there's no waiting until morning."

"Security of the nation? What's that got to do with me?"

"We need you to come with us, Mr. Wilson."

"Is this about the goddamn potato?"

"James, I don't want to hear you cussing."

"We don't owe you any explanation, Mr. Wilson. You're just coming with us now."

The tall guy behind the short guy pulled a gun from a shoulder vest. "Hey," I said. "Put that away."

"Come along. There's no reason to get dressed, Mr. Wilson. They'll have a uniform for you."

"Uniform? Where the hell am I going?"

"James! What did I say about cussing?"

"Maudine, there's two men out here from the FBI what are trying to arrest me."

"Not the FBI." The two guys looked at each other. "The National Security Agency," one of them said.

"Don't you fellas have a warrant?" I asked.

They started laughing.

*　*　*

"Maudine, I only got three minutes to talk."

"Praise Jesus! I just knew it was you when the phone rang, James. Where are you?"

"I don't know, Pumpkin. In some foreign country."

"Oh, Lordy."

"Seems like they was doing a wiretap on some terrorists and one of them called our house."

"Oh, Lordy, Lordy."

"Are you all right, Pumpkin?"

"You won't believe what happened after they took you away, James."

I was afraid to ask.

"Yesterday while I was cleaning the floor, there was this little man knocking on the door. He had on sunglasses even though it was raining outside. He couldn't speak English too good but he asks me to buy the potato."

"The potato? But..."

"I told him it was looking a little piqued, but he says he doesn't care. I say 'You might as well take it, it hadn't brung us nothing but trouble.'"

"Who was he?"

"I was scared to ask, but as soon as I hand him the potato he gives me this little black bag. Lord strike me down if I'm lying. After he leaves, I look inside and there's five thousand dollars!"

"Five thousand dollars?"

"The Lord didn't strike me down, so you know I'm not lying. I paid off the lady from the hospital, the light bill, and last month's rent. Jimmy and me are going to move in with Mabel Carter—she got that spare room—until I can find us another place to live."

"That's great, Pumpkin. But..."

"You just stay where you are, James. You know Mabel never did care for you and besides, it's crowded enough as it is."

I thought it over. Here I was getting three squares a day, and all they was doing to me was making me watch them flush the Koran down the toilet every once in a while. "It'd save on food money," I said.

"You know it would, James."

"I don't think I'm going to be able to call you again."

"It don't matter cause Mabel don't have no phone anyway."

So there it was. The reverend was right after all. The Lord do work in mischievous ways.

"I love you, Pumpkin."

"Praise God, James."

*After 17 rejections this story was finally accepted by
the* Iguana Review, *published in Greenbelt, MD
in their December 2008 edition. They published
literary works until the pandemic in 2020.*

Hairotica

"**W**hy do *you* think the man was with her in the shower, Virginia?"

Virginia squirmed in her seat. She regretted for the third time that she hadn't gone to the bathroom before walking into the glass and chrome offices of Marquis Marketing Research, LLC.

"I sure don't know. That's why I asked you," she said to the little white boy with the earring. "It's your movie."

"It's not a movie," said the white girl—well, Virginia thought it was a girl. "It's a commercial."

"I know it's a commercial. You told me that. I just don't know what it's a commercial for. Is it for sex? Because that's what it looked like to me."

That person—that girl—wanted to smile, but it looked like it hurt her to try. Virginia thought she might have little boobies under that man's jacket and shirt, but you never can tell. Why did she wear her hair so short?

"Virginia, tell us what *you* think the commercial is for," she asked.

Virginia knew they were both talking down to her, partly because she was old and wearing a dress from Goodwill, but mostly because she was a Negro. Not black, because her skin wasn't black, it was brown. Not African-American because, Lord knows, she wasn't from Africa, nor were any ancestors that she'd ever heard about. She didn't want to answer their question. Instead she raised an eyebrow at the two of them and shrugged.

"How about if we watch it again, this time with the sound on," the boy said, fiddling with the remote control in his hand. Oh, Lord, she didn't want to sit through it again, especially because she had to pee so bad.

The large flat screen on the wall came to life, and Virginia heard deep bass notes of a lub-dub like a heart beat. There was the same strange gold ripple that she now knew was really a close-up of a woman's hair—that woman who let herself be filmed naked in the shower sliding her hand down her tummy below her belly button, down to where, thank the Lord, the camera didn't follow. But Virginia knew what the woman was doing. She could tell by the way the woman's arm moved up and down. She could tell by the way the woman slipped her tongue through her painted lips and let droplets of water trickle into her mouth. Did these kids think she didn't understand? Or did they just want her to say it out loud? Is that what they were paying her thirty-five dollars for? Lord, what a world it had become.

Her legs. They reminded Virginia of that song, "Skinny Legs and All" by Joe Tex. Then the legs went up on tiptoes. Not a smart thing to do in the shower. A skinny girl like that could easily fall and hit her head on the tile. Soapsuds dripped down the inside of her thigh. Virginia figured it must be soapsuds. The camera followed the suds as they dripped down the curves of her skinny legs. Then there was some music. It sounded like a saxophone. Like maybe a tenor sax like John Coltrane played. Then the motion froze.

The boy with the earring played with the remote control. His hair was oily and slicked back like he was trying to look like a gangster, but Virginia knew he'd never seen a real gangster, just the Hollywood kind. Virginia had a grandson who hung around with real gangsters—the ones that had done time. This boy wouldn't last an hour in jail.

"What do you feel when you see this, Virginia?" he asked, not looking at her but at his purple plastic clipboard.

"What do you mean?"

"Does the woman look as if she's enjoying herself?" asked the person Virginia now thinks must be a woman. Her voice was too high to be a man's, but after all, there was a boy in her building who talked like that.

"You call it what you want," Virginia said.

The white boy and girl looked at each other. "Okay, Virginia," the boys said. "Let's watch some more."

There was steam from the water and it was difficult for Virginia to see what she was looking at. The saxophone music was slow and the lub-dub got faster. There was a round pink shape in the steam and Virginia could just make out the bottom of the woman's titties with the nipples sticking out. Lord forgive me, she thought, for looking at a white girl's titties for thirty-five dollars.

Then a man's hand came in, touching her under her boobies. The camera showed just a glimpse of his face, mostly his stomach. He looked like he must lift weights. Oh, Lord, you could see some of his hair that came from his privates. Now he ran a soapy hand near the woman's boobies. From behind his head Virginia could see the woman's face pressing against his shoulder. She had very blue eyes. White folks, she knew, liked blue eyes. The woman looked up then closed her eyes.

Virginia turned away from the screen toward the girl with the very short hair. She had tiny little glasses so Virginia couldn't see the color of her eyes. She should use a little makeup. She'll never get any man if she keeps dressing like one. Maybe she doesn't want a man. Virginia wondered if all commercials were made by people like these two.

"Pause it, Brandon," the girl said. She must be the boy's boss, Virginia thought, to speak to him in that tone.

"How does watching this make you feel, Virginia?" the girl asked. "Are the people in the commercial physically attractive to you?"

Virginia tried not to laugh. Did these white people have no manners? "Not to me. I suppose to somebody. The lady's a little skinny if you ask me. The man looks like that fella they're always showing on Access Hollywood. You know. I can't remember his name. Starts with a P. Pitt. Brad Pitt. Is that Brad Pitt?"

The two kids didn't say anything, but the boy wrote something on his pad.

"Does seeing these two people cause you to have any sexual thoughts or feelings?" the girl asked.

Now Virginia laughed to cover up her embarrassment—not for herself but for the girl who had to ask her such a question. "Honey, why in the world would you pay an eighty-two year old woman thirty-five dollars to answer a question like that? You look like a nice girl," Virginia lied, "and you must be smart or you wouldn't have such a good job, but you don't show much manners or sense."

The girl stood up. Her chin quivered. A wave of regret filled Virginia for speaking that way, although she thought maybe the girl needed to be spoken to like that. The girl gave Virginia a hard look, the kind Virginia had from white people plenty of times. Then the girl dropped her clipboard on the desk and walked out of the room, her shoes tapping like rain drops on a tin roof.

Now the boy turned toward Virginia. He looked to her like a very young, very awkward Hollywood gangster.

"Okay, then," he said finally. "Let's just watch the end of the commercial, Virginia. This is the part you didn't see the first time." He lifted up the remote.

There was a close up of the man's hand. He wrapped it around a pink plastic bottle that was sitting on shelf in the shower. It was tall and thin with a roundish pink lid on top, and it looked to Virginia for all the world like…well, she'd never seen a white man's, but that's what it looked like. The woman's hand covered the man's and together they brought it up to the woman's face, everything dripping wet. The woman licked her lips right near the bottle. The lub-dub got fast. Then the two of them must have squeezed the bottle because it suddenly shot liquid all over her hair. It kept shooting, but the man let go of the bottle and started rubbing it in the woman's hair. The saxophone slowed down, and there was a man's voice. "Wet Touch," it said. "The shampoo that comes with you in every bottle." Then the screen turned blue.

The boy put the remote down on the table. "After seeing the spot," he said looking at his clipboard, "would you say you would a) not buy Wet Touch, b) maybe buy Wet Touch, or c) definitely buy Wet Touch?"

"Son, I've used Head and Shoulders for forty years." She wondered what that boy put on *his* hair to make it shine like it did. "My niece does most of the shopping for me anyway. I can't carry much back from the grocery store by myself and she has a car. She always buys me Head and Shoulders. Do you have many more questions, because I need to use the ladies' room. Is there one handy?"

The boy put his pen on the clipboard and pushed it away. "Sure," he said. "Go down the hall past the receptionist. It's on the right."

She picked up her bag and followed his directions. The bathroom was dark red with posters all over the walls and smelled like perfume. There was someone in the last stall making sounds like she was throwing up. The stall door was open, and Virginia saw the girl in the man's suit.

"Can I help you, honey?" she asked.

The girl leaned back from where she was crouched by the toilet and slumped against the red tile wall. She wore black shoes that were so pointy they looked sharp. She found her little glasses on the floor and held them in her hands. "I get anxiety attacks," she said, breathing.

Virginia pulled some toilet paper off the roll and, with some effort, bent down to wipe vomit from the girl's chin. "Of course you do," she said. "With the kind of job you have, it's no wonder you make yourself sick."

"You have no idea," the girl said.

"Have you got a man in your life?"

The girl held on to the toilet seat and hoisted herself up. "What difference does that make?" Her face was pale, even for a white girl.

Virginia looked at the girl's hair. When Virginia was twenty-two she would have done anything to have a white girl's hair. She once tried to use a straightener. It was the worst smelling thing she knew, before or since. Later her pastor told her that it was a sin to try and change what God had ordained.

"Honey," she said, helping the girl stand, "maybe nobody ever told you, but you're a very pretty girl. You should let your hair grow. You got such nice hair. And you got blue eyes. Lots of people like blue eyes."

"Thanks."

Virginia could tell the compliments didn't mean a thing to the girl. Maybe the girl's mother never said anything nice to her. There were lots of mothers in Virginia's neighborhood who said terrible, cruel things to their daughters.

"I'll go back and answer some more of your questions," Virginia told the girl, "but first I have to pee."

"That's all right. You don't have to go back. When you leave here you can pick up your check from the receptionist."

"I don't want to get you into any trouble," Virginia said as she went into the next stall.

"It's just a fucking stupid commercial," she heard the girl say. Virginia thought that the girl was right but didn't say so. Then she heard the toilet flush and finally the click of the girl's shoes on the tile floor.

Virginia was glad they were paying her thirty-five dollars. She'd give it to her niece for groceries. She remembered they need some more Head and Shoulders.

*"Identity Crisis" was published in the print
version of* Fogged Clarity *in 2009.*

Identity Crisis

It took me a few seconds before I understood that the girl was talking to me. She stood on the step above where I was sitting, bent slightly, casting a shadow over my textbook.

"Joe!"

I looked up. She was a white girl. Her light brown hair was pulled back behind her ears with clips. She had large blue eyes and wonderfully smooth cheekbones.

"Joe?"

I have never been called Joe. I should have told her that then. I should have said that, even though all young African-American men must look alike, she was mistaken. But at that moment it seemed somehow unkind and unnecessarily rude, especially as she seemed so eager. And was so pretty.

I simply didn't know what to say.

"It's me, Wendy. You changed a flat tire for me last fall? On Morganton Road out near the reservoir?"

In high school I had taken honors classes where I was the only African-American in class. I was used to the way I was treated—with politeness and carefully measured acceptance. Never fully expressed, but always underlying, there was a quiet assumption that I was outsider, a representative of the slightly less-thans who had been given temporary entrance into the world of the slightly-more-thans. But the girls—and supremely the attractive ones—overtly regretted any attraction that they might have incited in me. They maintained a distance I had come to accept as inevitable.

"I don't know what I would have done if you hadn't come along."

"That's quite all right," I said, finding a voice. "I was glad to help." I told myself I was doing the right thing on behalf of 'Joe' and all African-American men. I was politely obliging, able to meet her standard of manners without being self-abasing.

"You didn't tell me you were a student here."

I held up my book. *Ethics of Psychology.*

"Psych major?"

"I can only hope," I said.

"Imagine that. If I had known you were here, I would have sent you a note. I don't think I ever really said thank you."

I shook my head, indicating suitable humility, hoping the interlude would end without embarrassment. "No problem," I said.

"Listen, Joe, could I buy you a cup of coffee or something? I feel like it's the very least I can do for you. It's cold out here anyway."

Her smile was distinctly not cold. It kept me from giving her the proper answer. "Maybe just a quick cup," I said. "I don't deserve any more than that."

I didn't.

We walked across the Quad to the Student Union Building, a distance of not much more than fifty yards. I ignored the part of me that was painfully aware of how entrenched I was becoming. Instead, I imagined the experience of walking with her as if it were a date, taking a measure of my real feelings for white women. My only girlfriends had been black, and all those of average attractiveness. None had as much of the look of a catalog model as this woman.

I held the door open. "Wendy, what's your major?"

She smiled again, looked directly at me, and I was struck by the softness and light of her eyes. "I can't make up my mind," she said. "I don't seem to have the brains for science, or the stomach for medicine. I was actually thinking of switching my major to psychology. Maybe you can tell me what I'd be in for."

I followed her to the Rathskeller where she immediately drew the attention of the eager student behind the counter. "I'd guess you'd be in for years and years of education," I said, "before you had enough letters after your name to get a decent job."

She laughed and ordered a latte. I took a cup of their house coffee, black, the least expensive thing on the menu board. We sat at a small wooden table near the window, beneath a poster of Bono.

"Is that what you want to do, Joe? Get a doctorate?"

"I just take it a semester at a time. Most of it depends on how much financial aid I get."

She blew across the top of her latte but put down the cup without drinking. "I hope you get all you need. You strike me as the kind of person who'd make a good therapist."

I was once again at a loss. I was desperately trying to construct a painless escape when a young woman, stocky and blonde, walked up to our table. "Susan," she said to Wendy, "did you ever find your phone?"

Wendy looked up. "I had to keep calling my own number from Frankie's phone," she said. "It turned out it was in my car. It had fallen in between the seats."

"Ah." The other woman, obviously perplexed, turned to me.

"Robin, this is Joe. Remember when I had that flat last fall? Joe is the guy who changed my tire. I had no idea he was a student here."

"Isn't that nice?" Her voice was flat. "I won't be back home until after dinner. I have to do laundry."

Wendy did what manners required. "Joe, this is Robin, She's one of my roommates."

I extended a hand that was reluctantly accepted. "Nice to meet you," I said.

"Sure. I suppose I'll see you later then." She shifted her shoulder strap and left, holding her Styrofoam cup with the hand that also held her books.

"She called you Susan." I immediately regretted the way I had said it, but she grinned, barely suppressing a laugh.

"This is really awkward," she said.

I waited.

"The thing is, it was dark and I wasn't sure what sort of person you might be. There are so many strange people out there these days. I gave you a different name. Just in case. My parents always taught me to be cautious with strangers. Especially…especially men, you know what I mean."

I knew what she meant.

"It's all right," I said. "I understand. There *are* strange people out there. My parents taught me the same thing. My name's not really Joe. It's David."

For a brief moment her grin remained, then it was lost. I hadn't meant to confuse her or confront her, but my words seemed to have upset some comfortable and unconsidered assumption.

I tried to come to her rescue. "But I'm glad to know your real name."

"Me, too."

I doubted that I would ever have another coffee with such a beautiful woman. "It's been nice to see you again," I said, rising. "Thanks for the coffee. I hope that makes us even."

She looked past me and stared out the window, where the sun was bright across the Quad, where the shadow of the library fell across the steps.

This piece of flash fiction was written to submit to a contest at the Carnegie Center for Literacy and Learning where I had been teaching Personal Storytelling. I had the idea for this piece around 2009 but never wrote it until the fall of 2024. It wasn't given an award for the contest and has never been published. It represents a bridge between periods when I was writing short stories.

Art for Art's Sake

Doc, why can't we see ourselves as others see us?

Arthur Degnan. Yes, that's the name on the insurance card. You'll want to spell it right.

Do I know why I'm here? No. Not for me. It's for him.

They really taught him. You see, at school they teach you to put yourself onto the canvas. Stroke by stroke. It's not paint, it's you, don't you see? You're taught to dig into the gut. Feel it. Extricate it. It's there so others can see. And judge.

Every agent, every gallery, every critic. I know the way the eye shifts just before they're about to shake their head and try to be polite. I know just how the emails start, "Dear Arthur, we…" before the feigned regret. They know best.

Twenty-seven years. He struggled, Doc. Arthur really did. So many canvasses, stacked up, painted over, painted over and over. His feelings, his burning.

It was a huge break for him. Being part of a show at Les Autres. Ever hear of it? The most prestigious gallery in the city. Twenty-seven years and part of a show at Les Autres.

Well, the review! Do you want me to read it? No, no trouble, I have it here in Art's wallet. *"Shattering. Excoriatable. Made us weep."* Blah, blah, blah. Well, I'll just skip to the end. That's the important part. Here it is, and I'll read it with a posh accent.

"…and also pieces hardly worth noting by someone named Arthur Debnan." Debnan. No, you had it spelled right the first time.

Too much sleeplessness, I guess, Doc.

I came downstairs very, very late last night. There he was, sitting in the kitchen, wearing my robe and PJs. It was like looking in a mirror. There he was, exactly like me in every way, but where was I? What happened to me in all this?

I knew he needed more than I could give. That's why I brought him here. So you can explain to him why we can't see ourselves as others see us.

Like several of these stories, this one began with using the title phrase as a writing prompt. It was published in 2025 in the online edition of The Brussels Review. *After writing it, I had an idea of turning it into a 10-minute play.*

A Grain of Salt

The bartender with the frayed flannel shirt pauses from drying a glass. "How's come you ain't eatin' your beer nuts, Frankie?"

Frankie looks up from his half-filled glass and pushes away the plastic cup holding the snacks." I can't eat peanuts no more. It's the salt."

The bartender lifts his eyebrows. "You turnin' into a health freak?"

Frankie grimaces and wipes his mouth on the paper napkin. "I went for a checkup this morning. I've been having them chest pains again. The doc said I'd better lay off the salt." He takes a sip. "Or else."

"What bullshit!" says the bartender. "My mother lived to be ninety and she ate nothin' but salt her whole life. Listen, my friend, you can't believe everything you hear. Especially from a doctor. They've all got their money tied up in them pharmaceuticals. I'll bet you didn't get outta that office without a prescription. Am I right or am I right?"

Frankie notices for the first time, and he'd been going to that bar for years, how the neon Coors sign over the bar and its reflection in the mirror broadcast two pink "Coors" into his beer. "No, not really," he says, mostly to himself.

"Frankie, Frankie, Frankie. You're a smart guy. When somebody like a doctor tells you something, you gotta take it with…I mean, he doesn't really expect you to never eat salt again. Hey, I read in an article once that people who eat health food cut their chances by fifty percent of ever enjoying themselves." He chuckles then shakes the drying towel. "Listen to me. You ain't gonna drop dead over beer nuts. I promise you that."

*　*　*

Frankie opens his eyes to see a man in a luminescent white robe standing at the foot of his bed. "Jesus Christ!" he screams.

The man laughs and the robe shimmers with the slight movement of his chest. "No, but that's a good guess," he says.

Frankie reaches to pull his blanket up but it's not there. "Who are you and how'd you get in here?"

The man doesn't answer for a moment. It looks to Frankie as if he's trying to decide how to answer. "You're dead, Frankie. There's just no nice way to say it."

As his eyes adjust to the brightness of the man's robe, Frankie starts to see the details of the man's face. He looks a little like Sister Sharon, his sixth-grade teacher—like he could be her male cousin. "Are you an angel?"

"I wish," the man says.

"A ghost?"

"Nah, thank God. I guess you could say I'm kind of a guide. I'm here to help you make a decision."

Frankie wasn't sure if it was because his eyes were getting used to the dark, but it looks like colored smoke is starting to turn to foam behind the spirit. "Am I really dead? he asks.

"What do you think, pal?"

"But...I mean, what happened? Last thing I can remember was...well, I remember Graduation Day at Blessed Mother Academy. No, wait. Now I remember gettin' married to Gloria. Then there was that fuckin' kidney stone. Hey, what are those beams coming out of your head?"

The spirit turns his head to look over his shoulders. His long, white hair sends tiny lights into the darkness as it moves. "Must be just something you're seeing. Do they look like scenes from old home movies?"

They kind of do, Frankie thinks. He squints his eyes and stares into the light. "Hey, that's the night Gloria kicked me outta the house. Is that what killed me?"

The spirit smiles and colored lights begin to appear behind his head. It isn't Sister Sharon who he really looks like, Frankie thinks. He actually looks a little more like Gloria, or like her brother—except she didn't have one.

"No, my friend," the spirit says. "It'll all catch up to you. You're fifty-eight. Well, you used to be fifty-eight. You were working at the GRM machine shop making drill bits. You had chest pains, remember that?"

The home movies seem to be getting bigger and brighter. And blurrier. Frankie starts to feel dizzy.

"You had a massive heart attack just a few hours ago. Your brain's blocked out all that trauma. Lucky you."

Frankie touches his chest. It feels ice cold. "Was it the salt that killed me?"

The spirit takes a step toward him and, as it looks to Frankie, sits on the bottom of his bed. Only there doesn't seem to be a bed.

"Salt?" the spirit asks, his eyes looking up for a long moment. "Hmmm. 'If salt loses its flavor, then how can it be seasoned?' Ever hear that one?"

The swirling lights around them seem to be swirling faster and Frankie has the feeling the two of them are moving together through a brilliant fog. He wants to grab on to something, but there isn't anything to hold. No, he changes his mind. It wasn't Gloria's brother, who she never had anyway. It's the bartender at Martelli's, except he's wearing a glowing robe instead of an old flannel shirt. Frankie scrunches his eyes and feels something familiar in what the spirit said. It takes a few moments to come to him. "Parochial school," he says. "Father Schulte's class, I think. I mean, that's from the Bible. Right?"

The spirit nods. "Matthew 5, verse 13. Do you know what it means?"

Frankie feels a weird sensation in his fingers, like his hands were mechanical cog wheels, turning with anything he touches, meshing into everything around him. Only there's nothing around him. He looks down but can't see his hands. He can't see anything but the shining fog swirling around the two of them.

"Yeah, I think it means that we're supposed to be good Catholics. Or maybe just good Christians," he adds, thinking the spirit might be a Protestant.

"Wrong!" says the spirit. "You've been taught a bunch of

nonsense, pal. Not your fault, of course. Still, there you are. It's supposed to make you think. Salt can't lose its flavor. It doesn't have any flavor. It's sodium chloride. Sodium chloride doesn't have any taste. You're the one with the taste. It's all going on in there." He points and Frankie feels a sharp touch on his forehead. "Jesus wanted us to understand that what we take for reality is a subjective experience, so we might realize who we really are. Get it?"

Frankie remembers that he barely graduated from Blessed Mother. He shakes his head. "Is this a test. I'm no good at tests. Am I going to hell?"

The spirit laughs and a shower of lights from his hair flow into the luminescence around the two of them. "No," he says. "You've just come from hell, Frankie. Only you're not Frankie any more."

"If I ain't Frankie, then who am I?"

"Sorry, pal. You're going to have to figure that one out on your own. You could've been working on it while you were alive. Well, no biggie."

The lights and the fog dim. The spirit shrugs, gets up from the bed that isn't there and begins to walk away.

"Wait! Where're you going? What's happening?"

The spirit's voice begins to echo. "Stuff to do," he says. "Anyway, good luck." He vanishes.

"Don't go away. Sorry I don't know nothin' about salt. Hey, you said you was going to help me make a decision."

A distant voice comes from the darkness. "Oh, yeah. Well, now you have an opportunity to work on developing your consciousness. Only most folks don't want to do that. They're just glad to sort of evaporate. Or you can hang around incorporeally and haunt some place you're attached to. I wouldn't recommend that. But that's up to you. Adios, amigo."

"What does incorporeally mean?" Frankie pleads.

There is no reply.

*   *   *

The young man sitting on a stool calls the bartender. "Hey," he says. "There's somethin' wrong with your Coors sign. It keeps flickering."

"I asked the Coors guy about it," the bartender says. "He can't figger it out. Nothin' wrong with it. He thinks the sign must be haunted."

"It's fuckin' annoying. It's driving me crazy."

The bartender has an edge in his voice. "It ain't gonna kill you. I can promise you that. Hey, how about some beer nuts?"

*After writing this story in late 2024, I contacted Sand
Pilarsky, the editor of the online magazine,* Piker Press.
*She had published many of my Warren stories between 2009
and 2013. She published this one on April 14, 2025.*

The Hole Truth

The weather was so beautiful I decided to call in sick. It was mostly a lie, but there really was something to it. I was pretty sick of my job. I had just had my Annual Review and gotten passed over again for a commendation in spite of totally deserving it.

So I shoved a couple of protein bars in my pocket and drove over to Andalusia State Park. It's an hour and a half or so from here, well off any regular roads. It's an unspoiled, beautiful wilderness and well worth the drive.

Hardly anyone was there in the middle of the week, which suited me just fine, because I wanted a break from people. I chose the Raven Cliff Loop Trail which winds down and up the mountain, and you eventually get a nice view of some river or the other.

I was glad I had taken the protein bars but, as I had forgotten to eat breakfast, I downed both of them in pretty short order. After about an hour on the trail, I also realized I had forgotten to go to the bathroom before I left, so I stepped off the path looking for a nice, private spot to pee. Not that there seemed to be anyone else in the entire park, but you just never know. I had just gotten to the part when I was shaking Old Mister Johnson dry when the whole thing happened. Or, rather, the hole thing.

And it happened so fast, it wasn't until a few seconds later that realized I had slipped down an embankment and slid into a hole. I mean a deep, dark hole. I later calculated it to be twelve-feet eight-inches deep. I was able to be that accurate because I had plenty of time to think about it. Hours and hours.

The sides were smooth rock with no possibility of getting a handhold and nothing to climb on top of. The fall hadn't done my knees any favor, and my old corduroy pants were pretty much ruined. I landed nice and hard against my phone, which cracked the screen, but there was no signal anyway. Not in the middle of Andalusia State Park.

Time goes pretty slowly when you're stuck in a hole with not much room to move. For a while I stared at the rock in front of me and the trees above me. That didn't hold my attention very long, so I started brooding about getting passed over for a commendation at work. Every day I went by cubicles where people have hung their plaques of commendations on the wall. And I know for a fact that I work as hard or harder than most of them. Brooding may be a good way to pass the time, but not much help in getting out of a hole.

After a few hours I heard voices.

One was a female and one was a male. And they were getting closer.

"Help!" I shouted.

"You hear something?" the girl said.

"I fell down a hole. Can you help me get out?"

"Sounds like somebody yelling 'help'," said the man.

"You think it's real?" she said.

"Yes, it's real! I'm down here in a hole!"

"I don't know," he said. "You never know these days. It might be some kind of scam."

"It's not a scam. I fell down the embankment and slipped into a hole, and I can't get out."

"You're not supposed to go off the trail," he shouted.

"I know that now," I said. "Look, do you have rope or something?"

By this time I could hear them clearly. They were about twenty feet above me, but I couldn't see them. "Why would I have a rope?" asked the man.

"Sounds a little bogus to me," she said. "I don't think we should get involved."

"Would you please call for help at least?" I could tell I sounded pleading.

"There's no cell service in the middle of Andalusia State Park," he said.

"Then please call somebody when you get back."

"Sure thing," he said. "It's just that we're heading out to the overlook for a picnic, and it might be a long time until we're where we can call anyone."

There was something he said that triggered me. "Ah, since you're going on a picnic, is there some food you could toss down to me. I don't know how long it's going to be before somebody comes to rescue me, and I'm starving."

It sounded like they were whispering.

"You'll have to speak up," I said. "I can't hear you."

"Well," said the woman. "When I packed this morning, I hadn't planned on someone asking us to share. We really only have enough for two."

"You sure?" I asked. "Not even a few chips?"

They started whispering again.

"Sorry," she said. "If we had known you'd be asking us, we would have brought more."

There wasn't much to say to that. "Okay," I said.

"Okay," said the man.

"Okay," said the woman, but she was already down the trail.

*   *   *

The light had moved a good bit from left to right in the trees above me by the time I heard voices again.

"Hey!" I shouted.

"Did you hear that, Sister?"

"No," said another voice.

"I swear I heard someone."

"Could it have been the voice of the Lord?"

"It sounded like someone shouting, 'Hey'."

"Probably not the Lord then," said the second voice.

"Hey!" I shouted again. "I've fallen in a hole. I need some help."

"Where are you?" said the first voice.

"Down here," I said, "over the edge of the trail. But don't get too close."

"What kind of help do you need?"

"Like maybe lowering down a rope. Do you have a rope?"

"I have a sash around my habit."

"How long is it?"

"What do you think, Sister?" she asked the other one.

"Maybe three feet. Would that help?" she shouted down.

I had to think a little bit about nuns and, frankly, I was feeling a little light-headed. "How about a really long rosary?"

There was silence and one said, "That's not going to work," while the other one said, "I don't think so."

"Okay," I said. "Then would you please go get somebody who can help. Like maybe there's a park ranger back at the parking lot."

"Did you see a ranger at the parking lot, Sister?"

"No, did you?"

"Well, do either of you have a cell phone?"

"There's no phone service in the middle of Andalusia State Park," one of them shouted down to me.

She was right, of course.

"We could pray for you," she added.

"Maybe four Hail Marys," said the other one. "Each."

"Thanks, Sister. If you can remember, please let somebody know I'm down here when you get back to where you have phone service."

"Will you help me remember, Sister?"

"Oh, may God help *me* remember! The other day I was looking and looking for my wimple and there it was in my hand."

"Well, I left Sister Tabatha's novena underneath her coif and forgot all about it."

"I can tell you what's even worse than that...," said the other one.

I never found out what was worse. They were out of range.

*　*　*

The forest was pretty much dark before anything else happened. I heard crunching feet and could see a sharp light jumping around in the tree tops.

"Ho!" shouted a voice.

"Hey!" I shouted back.

"Are you the guy who fell into a hole?"

My first impulse was to say something snarky. I was hungry, thirsty, sore and bored. But I realized I should try and be polite anyway. "Yeah," I said. "Who are you?"

"I'm Ranger Doug. You know you're not supposed to go off the trail."

"Oh, I know that now. But you guys should really build something over this. Or at least put up a sign warning people."

Ranger Doug laughed. "That's a good one. The Park Service doesn't even have enough money to pay me full time. And you have any idea what a sign costs these days? Here you go," he said tossing a thick rope over my head.

I felt something clipped to the end of the rope. I managed to get my cracked phone from my pocket and switched on the light. It was a manila envelope. "What's this?"

"That's just the standard disclaimer. You need to sign it to say you won't sue me, the Park Service, or the state if you get maimed or disfigured in the rescue attempt."

I took the paper out of the envelope and looked the thing over. "Disfigured?"

"Just standard procedure. I can't save you unless you sign it."

"I don't have anything to sign with."

"Ah, shit," said Ranger Doug. "Hold on." He pulled up the

envelope and fumbled around for a while before lowering it again.

"A crayon?"

"I picked it up in the parking lot the other day. You wouldn't believe the things people leave in the park. I once found part of an artificial foot in the port-a-potty."

I signed the form as best I could. The crayon was pretty dull. He hoisted it up again.

"Thanks," he said. "I'll just need to see two forms of photo ID."

I had to take a couple of slow breaths. "You can't see me down here in the dark. Why do you need photo IDs?"

"That's the rules. I can't rescue you unless I have two forms of photo ID. Like a driver's license and passport."

I reached around for my wallet and held my phone light to it. "How about a driver's license and a picture of me and my old girlfriend in a photo booth?"

"Was it a government-issued photo booth?"

I wondered if he was suspecting me of fraudulently falling into a hole. "I think so," I said. "It was taken at the State Fair last fall. I'm pretty sure the state government had to issue it, or they wouldn't have allowed it at a state fair."

He was quiet for a while, and I think I heard him kicking some stones around. "Maybe," he said finally. "You got anything else?"

"I have a membership card for Games Plus. It has a picture on it." It was a kid in front of a gaming console."

"Is the picture of you?"

I was awfully hungry and tired. "Does it have to be a current photo?"

"I don't think the regulation says anything about recent a photo it has to be."

"Then it's me," I lied.

"Okay," he said finally. I think he might have been hungry and tired, too. He tossed down the rope. I put my license and my Game Plus card into the envelope. He pulled it back up, looked them over, and then threw It down again. "Here we go."

"Okay," I said. "Hold on tight, I'm climbing up."

I got about four inches.

"How much you weigh?" Ranger Doug said, sounding like he could barely talk for straining.

"194," I said, giving myself some leeway for not eating anything except a couple of protein bars that whole day.

"Geezis, this isn't going to work. I'm going to have to call Search and Rescue. They aren't going to be happy about it. I think they have bowling league tonight."

I heard some squawking from his walkie-talkie, and he moved up the path where I couldn't hear. I thought I caught him saying 'some big fat guy,' but I'm not sure.

It was about an hour later when I heard a helicopter roar and it shone Hollywood-type lights all over until they hit me in the face. Then they lowered a chain with a harness that I had to strap under my arms. I pulled the buckles extra tight. I had no desire to get maimed or disfigured.

Up I went, hitting a few times on the sides of the hole but, as I said, my brown corduroy pants were already pretty much ruined. They let me down where the whole thing started (or should I say the hole thing?) and Ranger Doug grabbed me.

"I'm really sorry about this," I said to him once I had disentangled myself from the harness. "Sorry I caused a big hassle for everyone."

We started back up the path toward the parking lot. "They'll probably close the park for good after this," he said. "The Park Service has been running in the red for years, and they're always looking for an excuse to cut the budget. It'll mean me losing my job, but it's about time I got myself a new career. I always thought I'd enjoy being a rocket scientist. I mean, how hard could *that* be?"

It was on the news the next day and, although I didn't get fired for taking the day off, I did get docked for a day's pay for lying about being sick.

About a month or so later, I got a special delivery letter from the Governor. He was thanking me for saving taxpayers thousands of dollars a year for my part in the closing of Andalusia State Park. He said the state was selling the land to a developer who planned to put in cluster housing and a water park and would bring cell service to the whole area. It was going to be a windfall for the taxpayers.

With the letter was a certificate suitable for framing. It was an official commendation for a job well done. I hung it on the wall of my cubicle.

Written in the autum of 2024, this story was published in
The Brussells Review *in the Summer 2025 print edition.*

Please Help Yourself

There was no receptionist, only an extremely messy desk with an empty plastic bowl that once must have held candy and a hand-written sign offering, "Please help yourself." Next to that was another—also hand-written—sign that warned, "Wait until the doctor calls you in." Above the two signs and the extreme mess was a Felix the Cat clock on the wall, ticking so loudly I wouldn't have been surprised if the other offices in the building had complained.

A couple of days before I had received a very glossy, very colorful mailer offering a free introductory session with P. Diddle Dean, MD, Psychiatrist. I had for some time been wrestling with the Old Depression/Anxiety Thing, and I figured a free introductory session couldn't hurt. I decided to make an appointment, despite wondering, after studying the postcard for a while, what sort of first name a man might have if he chose to publicly use a middle name like Diddle?

There was no one else in the waiting room, but I knew from a previous visit to a mental doctor some years before that these guys didn't like their patients to get a look at each other coming and going, either for confidentiality or to keep them from scaring each other. Eventually the top portion of a man with heavy-rimmed glasses above a bow tie and a pink carnation popped out from the doorway. "Come in," he called, just as the sign had predicted.

The room I entered was so dark it took a few seconds for my eyes to adjust. All the walls were covered in drapery. There was a captain's chair, obviously for the doc, and a couch in the style of how cartoonists draw a shrink's office. The only light was a miniature Victorian lamp on a side table.

He made a gesture toward the couch. "Please make yourself comfortable. I'm Doctor Dean," said Doctor Dean.

The phrase, "May I call you Diddle?" came to my lips, but I knew that it wasn't the time or place to kid around. This guy had spent some ungodly number of years in school, and depression/anxiety is truly no laughing matter. So I lay down, asking first if it was okay for me to keep my shoes on.

"Please relax," he said, almost as if it were a command. "Your intake form said you've been suffering from depression and anxiety and trouble sleeping."

"Not only did my intake form say that," I replied, "but I'll say it, too. It's pretty awful. I'm tired like all the time except when it's time for bed. I feel like I'm scared of something, but I don't know what. And I feel guilty about all kinds of things."

"Uh huh," he said, as if he were thinking about something else. "Let's take a look at you."

He must have had some sort of remote control in his hand because just then the curtains on all four walls retracted, revealing four gigantic mirrors on all sides. It was like finding myself in a sideshow Hall of Mirrors. Every time I moved my head to look at another mirror, about sixty of me moved their heads.

"Whoa!" I said. "That's weird."

"I'd like you to relax," he said, again as if I'd better do it or else. He started skooching his heavy captain's chair up to where my head was on the couch.

I stopped moving my head around to look at the mirrors, but I kept moving my eyes, and it was crazy to see all the doctors moving their chairs. I never knew just how ugly my nose was until that moment. Or how I really was thinning on the top of my head like my barber kept insisting. I closed my eyes.

"Please open your eyes," ordered the doc. When I did, I saw he was holding up a pocket watch, I swear, just like in the movies. "Just look at the watch," he said. "And try to relax."

What else was there for me to do? I had taken the morning off from work, driven all the way downtown, and committed to pay a small fortune for parking. I watched the watch as he dangled it back and forth and, damn it, I did start to feel relaxed. I forgot all about the mirrors. It was nice and quiet in there—only a very faint ticking of Felix from the waiting room. And the couch was pretty comfy. Plus I had only gotten a few hours of sleep the night before. I felt myself starting to drift off.

"Are you trying to hypnotize me?" I asked.

"No," he said. "I'm trying to un-hypnotize you."

The moment he said the word 'you' I felt an icy shock to my face. There was a stream of the coldest water known to man shooting out from the carnation in his lapel, aimed at my forehead. "What the fuck?" I shouted.

I wiped my face with my hand and then noticed something really bizarre. The mirrors were still there, and in them I could see the doc, the chair, the couch, the tiny Victorian lamp, but not me. I looked down at my hands and for one panicky moment I didn't see them. Or the rest of me. I could feel my heart pounding like I was in some serious trouble. I lifted myself up to look into the mirrors on the walls. I definitely wasn't there. "What the fuck happened?" And I'm not sure that my voice didn't crack like a twelve-year old.

"You're all right," said Dr. Dean. "Just lie back and close your eyes."

I did what he said.

"What do you feel?"

"Scared as shit," I said.

"Why is that?" he asked.

"I feel like I disappeared."

"Can you feel your body?"

I wiggled my hands. "Yep."

"Can you tell me where you are?"

I figured this was a standard shrink question to sort out the truly disturbed. "In the office of Dr. P. Diddle Dean, Psychiatrist, lying on a couch with my eyes closed."

"Do you know that for sure?"

"What do you mean 'for sure'? Of course I do."

"How do you know that?"

I opened my eyes. I could see my hands again. "Well, I don't know. Common sense, I suppose. Why can't I see myself in the mirrors? How do you do that?"

He ignored the question. "So you know that you're here, even though you can't see any reflection of you?"

"I have to admit, Doc, it's damn disconcerting to look into all those mirrors. For a second I couldn't even see my own body. I don't know what all that has to do with my not feeling like myself lately."

The drapes started moving again, and in a moment all the mirrors were covered. "Somehow," he said, "you had sense of yourself, even though the reflections of you disappeared. What if I amputated your legs?"

I laughed—pretty nervously, really hoping he was kidding.

"And your arms. What if I erased your memory? What if I got rid of your depression? Would you still be you?"

"Well," I said trying to laugh again, "next to all that, shock therapy doesn't sound so bad."

"You didn't answer the question."

I had to think what he asked. "Well, I'd be one damn confused quadriplegic. But if you got rid of my depression, I guess I'd be a happy, confused quadriplegic."

"But would you still be you?"

"What do you mean?"

"When you couldn't see yourself in the mirror, did you still have a sense of your own existence?"

I sat up. "This is getting all a bit too deep for me, Doc."

He stood up. "Okay. That's the end of our session. If you'd like to make another appointment, you can do so through the portal on my web site." He handed me a business card.

So that was that. Of course, I chucked the business card. A few days later I saw my regular primary care guy and he gave me a scrip for an anti-depressant. In a month and a half I was feeling like my old self again.

Once, about nine months after all this, I was in Dr. Dean's neighborhood and went into the lobby to see if he was still listed in the directory. He wasn't. Instead, there was a tattoo-removal clinic in that office.

But the thing—I mean, the really big thing— is that many years later I started thinking about my session with P. Diddle Dean. It was after I got diagnosed with fourth-stage cancer. I was told that three months would be very optimistic.

I remembered how, in spite of disappearing from those mirrors, I had still been there. And I knew it. And now, in spite of disappearing from all the reflections of myself in the world, I'm just beginning to know something about who I truly am. I'm sorry for all the years I wasted in between.

Thanks, Dr. Dean, wherever you are.

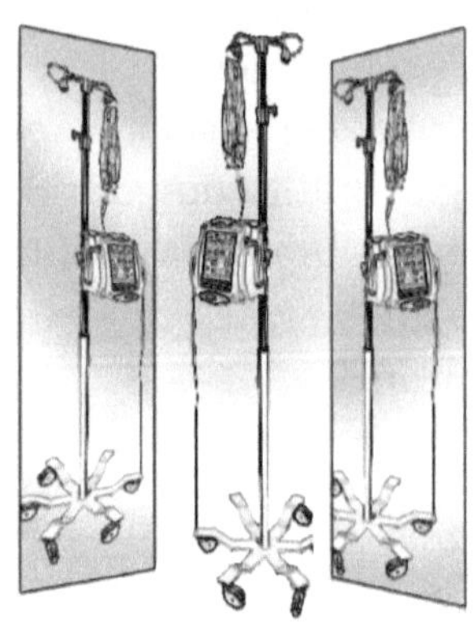

Resonation

Friday, October 18

Henry had been worried he might feel conspicuous carrying such a large bouquet of roses on the subway. But it was still early enough on a Friday evening that the car was full of late commuters and people heading out of town for the weekend, and everyone seemed as self-absorbed as usual.

He stood holding on to the strap with one hand, the flowers in the other, watching a woman in a plain white dress sitting near him. She seemed fully occupied with a book, and Henry felt he wouldn't be noticed if he kept staring. She was not especially a classic beauty. Her nose, he thought, might be a little pointed. Her light brown hair, pulled back at the sides and clipped behind her ears, was thin and frizzy. But he wasn't able to look at anything else.

Her dress came to her knees, and she was wearing what looked to Henry to be ballet shoes, white like her dress and cross-tied around her ankles. It didn't occur to him to wonder if she were a dancer, nor wonder if she were thin, tall, or guess at her figure. He was preoccupied with something else about her. Something he couldn't define.

Henry thought it might have been the strange human ability of sensing being watched, but the woman finally glanced up from her book, looked up to Henry and smiled for a moment. He tried to return her smile, but it was so brief he wasn't sure if she had been smiling at him or at a thought of her own. It didn't seem to matter. He felt a rush in his chest from meeting her eyes.

At the first stop, a burly man holding a hardhat got up from next to the woman and Henry threw himself into the vacant seat without thinking. She didn't seem to be paying attention. He looked at the book she was holding and for a moment thought to ask about it. That seemed like a pick-up line, so he spoke without forethought. "Hey," he said, "would you like to have these flowers?"

She looked up. There were those eyes again and the rush in his chest they caused. "Are you talking to me?" she asked in a voice that sounded oddly familiar.

"Absolutely. I'd like to give these to you. I promise there are no strings attached."

She laid her book in her lap. When she took the bouquet, she pulled at the string that wound the stems together, and raised an eyebrow at him. "Are you sure?" She smiled again.

Henry half-laughed to try to relieve his awkwardness. "I'll tell you the whole story if you promise you won't feel sorry for me."

"Jilted at the altar?" He was suddenly aware of her complexion, her cheekbones, and the shape of her mouth.

"Almost," he said. "It was supposed to be a blind date. A woman I met online. I was on the way to her apartment when I passed a flower stall. I thought she might find it funny if I brought her an oversized bouquet of roses. We'd been doing a lot of joking around through messaging on the dating site. When I got to her building, there was no apartment with that number. I checked back on the app, and I hadn't made a mistake. Or, actually, I had. The account had been deleted. I'm thinking now she was probably a kid with a bunch of fake photos. My own fault, I guess."

"I think the fault's hers, not yours."

"Well, I'm not so sure, but kind of you to say. I walked around the block feeling stupid for a while and finally decided to go back home. I don't know why, but I had a sudden hunch to give them to you."

"Thank you. They're beautiful. It's funny, but I've been thinking about hunches today. Are you the kind of a person who usually acts on hunches?"

He was nervous. "Only on certain occasions," he said, trying to smile. In contrast, the woman seemed confident and casual, and her openness caused the same tugging at his chest as her eyes had done. "I'm sorry if I interrupted your reading."

The book in her lap was small with a plain green cover, a single gold stamp on the cover. RESONATION. "It's a sort of memoir from the nineteenth century," she said. "About a boy growing up in Northern India. But it's really about what he learned from all these remarkable people he met in his life."

"Remarkable people? Like Hindu mystics?" he asked. "That sort of thing?"

She scrunched her face. "Not so much. But full of things out of the ordinary. Mostly it's about his search to find meaning in a life that seemed to have little meaning."

He wondered if he were falling in love at first sight. The subway began to screech into its next stop, and he knew he had to leave in spite of this ridiculously irrational feeling. "Henry," he said, offering his hand. "Henry Abbot."

She laid down the book, switched the roses to her left hand and offered him her right. "I'm afraid it's not so simple with me. I'm officially Elizabeth, Beth to my family, Libby to college friends, Liz to my co-workers."

They shook hands as he stood. "Who would you like to be to me?"

"How about Lizzie?" she said after a moment.

"Okay, Lizzie. I hope we meet again sometime."

"I hope so, too. Thank you for the roses, Henry."

He left the subway car, feeling as if his heart was breaking.

Saturday, October 26

He had arrived at the restaurant ten minutes early. The entrance was below the sidewalk by a few steps so he decided to stand against the railing to watch for her arrival. When fifteen minutes passed, he did what he promised himself he wouldn't. He pulled out his phone and flipped back for the third time through his messages. The embarrassment of getting stood up at his previous rendezvous-to-be was still fresh.

I'd like to buy you lunch to thank you for the flowers you gave me last Friday. Could we meet this Saturday? Warmest regards, Lizzie

And there she was. He saw her crossing the street into the block. She was all in white again, stretch pants and a loose shirt that came down to her thighs. Purse over her shoulder. Still in the ballet slippers. She was looking at the ground, her shoulders slumped, and her stride slow. He wondered if she sensed his staring again because she suddenly looked up.

He waved and she waved back. He watched her walk, wondering for the first time if she might be a dancer. She wasn't thin or tall enough, he thought, but when she saw him her posture changed and her step became light.

"Am I late?" She shouted when she was closer.

"Just barely," he shouted back.

They shook hands and he brought up the first of the many things he had on his mind. "How did you find me?"

"Truthsearch.com," she said. "I had to pay 20 dollars to get your phone number. Does that sound like stalking?"

"If it does, I'm guilty, too. I looked you up, too, from your number. You live here in Chestnut Hill."

She pushed open the door. "Let's go in. I know I kept you waiting."

He started to say something polite like 'Not at all,' but a woman with a nose ring and heavy eye makeup led them to their seats. "Chestnut Hill is actually an old address," she said, sliding into a booth seat. "I'm now living in Whitemarsh with my sister and brother-in-law."

"How's that working out?" he asked. Instead of picking up his menu, he focused once on her eyes, wondering what it was that affected him so profoundly.

She sighed. "Living with relatives? Some things good, some not so good. Like life."

"It sounds like there's a story in there, but I won't press you." He changed the subject. "How's the food here?"

"Well, I guess it's the same answer. Some good, some not as good."

"Like life?"

They smiled at each other.

The woman with the nose ring appeared at their booth, looking as pleasant as she could manage. She slid a pair of ice water glasses at them and took their order.

When they were alone again, and in the silence that followed, he mustered the courage to bring up the second thing on his mind. "I also stalked that book you were reading, *Resonation*. How much do you know about it?"

"What do you mean?"

He picked up a spoon from the table and stirred absently the ice in his glass. "Well, like about the author?"

"Govinda Ahmad Khan?"

He turned away, toward the window with bars that looked out on the bottom of the sidewalk. "That wasn't his real name. He didn't grow up in Northern India. He wasn't Indian at all. He was Canadian. I guess in the nineteenth century you could get away with a whole lot more than you can today." She said nothing and he turned back to her eyes. "I probably shouldn't have brought this up. Obviously you find some value in the book. I feel like I'm being a first-class asshole."

"No, actually I found out all that."

"And it doesn't bother you that he was a fake? That the book is a fake?"

"Well, I'm not sure I'd call it a fake."

"If that's not a fake, then it's cultural appropriation. It's just that it bothers me when people try to speak for other

150

people who they know nothing about. It's wrong. I'm sorry. I should just get down from my soapbox and stop spoiling a delightful lunch."

"You're not spoiling anything."

"Well," he said, stirring his ice water again. "I think I am. Anyhow, what difference does it make? That book is almost two hundred years old and the author is long gone."

"But don't you think that's the thing about written literature? It still has power to affect readers long after the author is dead. It's like ripples that keep on going, reaching out over time and space."

He smiled. "You're an idealist."

She smiled back. "I wish I were."

He waited for her to speak. When she didn't, he felt the warmth leave the situation. He was feeling guilty about being so officious. It wasn't the way to make a good impression. "Of course, I didn't read the book."

"You probably wouldn't, now you think it's a fake."

"Probably not." He struggled to change the subject. "Hey, I notice that you wear dance shoes. Are you a dancer?"

She smiled again, but this time it looked to him as if she were doing it with effort. "No, not a dancer. I was never a professional or anything serious. I used to take a class at the Arts Center that they should call Ballet for The Clumsy. Dancing is something I love but I'm terrible at it. If I were really an idealist, I would probably believe more in myself."

The waitress plopped down their sandwiches. "I think this is yours," Lizzie said to Henry. They switched plates, looking at each other, sharing a thought about their waitress. "The food is better than the service," she said.

They ate in silence, but there was something he had to say before it seemed too late. "Lizzie, when I first saw you last Friday on the subway, I got a feeling—like a vibe from you." He wasn't being careful with his words. "I had a sense you were a person I wanted to get to know. I hardly know you, but I've decided I like you already."

She stopped eating. "The truth is, Henry, it meant a lot to me when you sat down next to me and gave me those flowers. I've been— sort of struggling lately. Hard to put into words. It's actually been a long time, I guess, since I felt I've been noticed. And there was something in your eyes I felt, too. I want to get to know you better, too. But I better tell you the truth."

Her words struck him like a stomach punch. He hadn't seemed to be having good luck with women lately. He braced himself. "Please do," he said.

"On Monday, I'm going to Texas for a four-week program at the Menninger Clinic. It's a psychiatric hospital."

He had been prepared for something worse. "Oh," he said. "I mean, are you all right? No, of course. You wouldn't be going there if you were all right."

"I had to quit work last year over some emotional-slash-psychological problems. I went through some really tough times. Self-harm and places I don't want to talk about. Without a job I finally had to move in with my sister. No insurance at that point, of course. My sister paid for me to go to a doc. And she's paying for me to go to Menninger. So, you see, I'm kind of a mess."

He touched her hand. "Lizzie, I don't know what to say to you other than I'm really sorry you've had to go through this. Will you be coming back here afterwards?"

"Yes. I don't really have anywhere else to go."

There was more silence. He ate some of his sandwich and without giving it a thought, heard himself say, "Can I see you again then?"

She drew in a long breath. "The thing is, I've had some bad experiences with men who wanted to rescue me."

He looked out across the restaurant as if he were searching for inspiration. There was that feeling in his chest again. He shook his head. "I don't think that's what I want."

"What is it that you do want?"

He decided he would consider his words before speaking. "You know what the title of your book means? It's a nineteenth-century form of the word 'resonance.' It's like this. I play the guitar. Well, I guess I play the guitar the same way you dance. I've messed around since I was a teen-ager, but I've never gotten really good at it."

She said nothing. Henry felt she was looking at him as if there were something in his eyes she wanted to find.

"On a standard six-string guitar, the notes go E-A-D-G-B, and the highest note is another E. But, if you pluck the low-E, the high-E starts to vibrate. None of the other strings do. Only the two that are tuned the same, even if they are in a different octave. You can't tell that's going to happen just by looking at the two strings. But once you notice the resonation, you know.

She smiled and he relaxed—except for the strange sensation in his chest. "And how does that relate to me?"

"Well, that's the thing. I can't explain it. It's like there's something about you that I can feel in myself. I felt it the moment I saw you on the subway."

"Was it pity?"

The absurdity made him laugh in spite of himself. "I'm sorry to laugh," he said. "I don't know what to call it, but it was the opposite of pity. Look, I truly am sorry that you're in a bad place right now. But look at what you're doing. You're doing something fucking courageous to get better. You're even reading a book about finding meaning in life. You're saving somebody's life — yours."

This time when she smiled, it creased a dimple in her cheek.

"Will you have your phone with you for the next four weeks?" he asked.

"Actually, I have no idea. I've never done anything like this before."

"Email?"

She shrugged.

"Before you go, would you be willing to text me the physical address of this place in Texas?"

She laughed. "You are a kind person, Henry. Please think over carefully if you really want to get involved with a woman like me."

For what seemed like far too long, he didn't say anything. He looked back out the window. "I already am," he whispered.

Sunday, November 17
To: Henry Abbot
North 12th Street, Apt 7
Philadelphia, PA 19130

Dear Henry,

Thank you for your note and all your kind words. Hearing from you meant more to me than all the help this place has provided so far.

Since I arrived, I've been kept busy with a daily schedule (that they present me with) of therapy sessions—group and individual—and a kind of a smorgasbord of different modalities like bio-feedback and EMDR. (You can look that one up if you don't know what it is.) All this is to apologize for not writing back to you until now.

Of course, all the attention has felt good, but I just hope that in itself is worth what my sister is paying for me to be here. So far, they haven't uncovered some magic bullet that will immediately take away the horrible pain I've been in.

But here's the strange and beautiful thing: I think I'm uncovering it myself. Well, with your help. I honestly don't know how my problems are supposed to connect to the truly shitty life my sister and I had growing up. My gorgeous sister has a devoted husband and a brilliant kid and a lucrative career, so if it's our past that's supposed to be haunting me, she escaped it. Or, at any rate, that's how it looks on the outside.

The day I met you on the subway, I had gone downtown for a dance workshop, but I found I just wasn't up for it. Instead

I spent the day on a bench in Rittenhouse Square feeling invisible to everybody passing by. I hadn't had anything to eat, and by the end of the day I felt a little light-headed. Maybe that was part of the reason I started paying attention to a series of hunches. The first one took me into a hole-in-wall used bookstore on Sansom Street. The second was to notice this little green book tucked away on a bottom shelf. I took it to a sandwich shop and started reading.

You already know what it's basically about—a search for meaning in life, set in 19th century India. I related so closely to the protagonist in the story that I got totally absorbed. I was on the subway reading about an encounter the main character has with a stranger near a shrine. The stranger tells him, "One day, may you meet someone who can show you to yourself."

That was when you offered me your flowers.

For a long time, I thought it was simply being paid attention to after a whole day of feeling invisible. But now I think it was more than that. I think that in some way I can't understand, you might be able to show me to myself. You seem to see me more clearly than I've been able to see myself for a long time.

When you introduced yourself on the subway, you said, "Who would you like to be with me?"

I think the answer is, finally, I'd like to be the one I somehow lost.

I'm flying back to Philadelphia next Monday. I would very much like to see you again, if you aren't afraid of all my psychological baggage. If you are, I totally understand.

Warmest regards,

Lizzie

Wednesday, November 21

To: Ms. Elizabeth Kiner
c/o "In Crisis" Program
The Menninger Clinic
12301 S. Main Street
Houston, TX 77035

Lizzie,

After an hour of searching last week, I found a copy of *Resonation* online and bought it (for a ridiculous shipping charge). It sat on my night stand for a couple of days before I gave it a try. I finally decided that I had spent more on it than I really could afford. And I had done that recently with a humongous bouquet of roses, and look what that brought me.

I read the book straight through, hours in bed one night. I began to realize what you meant saying you weren't concerned if it were a true story or not. My initial judgment was way too shallow. I don't know why the author cloaked his ideas in a distant, mysterious culture. Maybe to get people to take him seriously. But I don't think the point of the book has anything particularly to do with India or Hinduism.

Unlike you, up to now I've been able to push aside the nagging, seemingly unanswerable questions that should be brutally apparent to all human beings. As you know, the author (whoever he was) doesn't easily let the reader get away with that. But, also as you know, it's not just a book intended to deconstruct our mental structures. I, too, identified with the protagonist (whoever he is supposed to be) and his developing a sense of meaning for his life.

Honestly, in some way I can't explain to you, this book wouldn't have meant much to me if I hadn't met you. But, as it is, I feel like a low E string that's been set into vibration by a high E.

I have no worries about your psychological baggage. In fact, I doubt it's baggage at all. You are incredibly courageous and insightful. And, more than that, I think you can help show me to myself. I have no words that are adequate to thank you. I called your sister and asked if it would be all right for me to meet you at the airport on Monday.

If you've forgotten what I look like, I'll be the guy with a ridiculous bouquet of roses.

With love,

Henry

I submitted this story to several literary journals, although I never expected any of them to be interested in publishing a story in parable form. Of course, my hunch was correct. This form of literature was far out of fashion.

What was in fashion at the time, though, was the cultural fascination in the seemingly sudden availability of artifical intelligence. I came across many references to articles pondering its potential to rival human consciousness.

The Parable of the Clockwork Man

Once upon a time, in a time no one can remember, and in a place that shows on no map, there was an intelligent and ambitious man named Alab. When he was young, Alab became apprenticed to a woodworker. Because of his aptitude and hard work, Alab soon developed more skill than his teacher, and he became known as the finest woodworker in the land. But after a time, Alab grew bored with the acclaim and with woodworking itself.

One day he decided to quit his trade and apprenticed himself to a clock maker. He applied himself to this trade as he had done to woodworking and eventually became the town's finest clockmaker. Once again, at the height of his career, Alab felt restless and announced that he was abandoning clockmaking forever.

Finally, Alab became an apprentice to a doctor, learning everything he could from the master physician. After several years, Alab's teacher offered Alab the position of the town's doctor, saying the apprentice had surpassed him in all skills and knowledge of medicine. For a while, Alab felt challenged by the continual variety of cases presented to him, but eventually his inevitable restlessness overcame him.

By this time, Alab was a man of middle age. He realized he was not only bored, but lonely as well, as his ambitions and hard work had left no time to acquire friends, let alone a spouse to be his helpmeet. One evening, while sitting alone in his garden after his evening meal, a thought came to him.

"I know more about the human body than likely is known to anyone. With my consummate craftsmanship in woodworking and my superb skill clockmaking, I believe I could construct an automaton, a replication of a human being which could serve as my own son and a companion in my old age."

Such was Alab's great intelligence that, after reclusing himself for an entire year, he actually created a mechanical man run entirely by clockwork and skillfully shaped in the finest wood to resemble a human being. "I will name him Salil," he said, "and teach him all the things I know. That way we will be able to engage in lively conversations on the subjects that interest me."

For many years, Alab enjoyed teaching Salil and discussing with him all the thoughts that occurred to him. One morning, however, in the time usually given to their conversations, Salil said to him, "Father, as you know, I am very grateful to you for creating me, but now that I know more about you, I'm no longer content to be a mere clockwork boy. I would like to become a real human being."

Alab was at first disturbed by this, but, because of a desire to please his son and a desire to take on a new a challenge, he set himself the task of making Salil into a real man. He researched, investigated, and pondered deeply into the matter. One day he told Salil, "My son, from what I have read, it appears that the method of transmuting yourself into a true human being is for you to devote yourself to the service of humanity."

"That sounds simple enough, Father," said Salil. "What does the service of humanity entail?

Alab thought for several moments and then gave his son this advice. "Every morning you must walk through town, offering to help those who are tired to carry their burdens. In the afternoons, go to the farms and make yourself available to help care for animals and to plow fields."

So the very next day, Salil did as his father suggested. In a very short amount of time, he became known as a great helper to one and all. Because he was made of wood, he never tired and only required occasional winding to keep him working. He always refused compensation for his efforts because, as he told people, "I have no need for food since I run entirely on clockwork."

But after a year of devoting himself to the service of humanity, Salil still had not become a real human being. "Father," he said one day, "might there be a more effective way that I can become real? I fear that the method you gave me is not working."

With great sympathy for his son's disappointment, Alab once again devoted himself to learn how Salil might attain his goal. After much thinking about the qualities that distinguish human beings from inanimate objects, he told him, "My son, it has occurred to me that only humans are capable of love. In order to become real, you must learn to love and be loved by others."

"I will do as you suggest, Father, for my desire to be real hasn't diminished. If anything, it has become greater. But, as I am still just a clockwork boy, you must teach me the meaning of love."

"Well," Alab told him, "love may seem like a difficult concept to grasp, but you may conceive of it as a deep and consistent attraction to someone else."

Salil pondered this statement. "How then shall I become the recipient of such deep and consistent attraction?"

"That is for you to discover," said Alab.

So Salil set off to become as attractive as he could, never missing an opportunity to develop an attraction to someone else. But, after another year of effort, he returned to his father, lamenting, "Father, I found many people who seemed to me to be worthy of attraction, but all of them eventually said to me, 'Salil, you are a very nice clockwork boy, but we can't love you because you are not real.' It appears that my goal of being a real human is impossible."

Alab hung his head and sighed. "Throughout my entire life I have been able to learn anything I set my mind to, but I'm afraid this challenge is simply too difficult. But there yet might be one hope left for us. I have heard of a man named Hakim Jidi who lives at the very top of a rugged and desolate mountain. He is reputed to help others who are in desperate circumstance. Perhaps if we present him with this problem, he will be able to solve it."

So the two set off the next morning to find the mountain home of Hakim Jidi. After many difficulties, they reached the summit of the tall mountain where stood the humble shack of Hakim Jidi. The wind howled all around them, but the sage came out and greeted them. "If you have traveled this far to see Hakim Jidi," he said, " you must be in great need. Here, rest yourself beside my hut and tell me how I might help you."

So Alab told Hakim Jidi about his life and how he came to construct a clockwork boy. Salil, for his part, recounted all his efforts to become real and beseeched the wise man for his aid. "What makes you think you are worthy to become a real human being?" asked Hakim Jlli.

So Salil told him about the wonderful qualities his father had built into him and all that he was capable of doing. "That is most impressive," said the sage. "Can you also fly?"

"I don't know," said Salil. "I have never tried."

"Perhaps now you can try," said Hakim Jidi.

And before anyone could prevent him, Salil went to the edge of the mountain top and threw himself into the wind. For a moment he was tossed in the currents but then plummeted into the valley far below, too far away for the two men to hear the sound of wood and metal smashing into bits.

"You fiend!" cried Alab, staring into the abyss. "Author of all misfortunes! What have you done? My life's work is destroyed. I will never be able to create another clockwork man. A thousand curses upon you. Why did you ask him to fall to his destruction?"

"Your request for help was misaligned," said Hakim Jidi calmly. "You should have come to ask my help to make *you* into a real human. If you were truly real, there would be no need for your mechanical man to become real."

"To Satan with you!" shouted Alab. And, hanging his head in his hands, he ran down the mountain continuing to hurl curses upon the head of Hakim Jidi.

When he returned to his own town, Alab continued to try to minister to the health of the local people, but because he was consumed with anger and bitterness, people began to avoid him. Eventually, Alab's anger turned into melancholy and soon no one, not even himself, could stand his company. The words of Hakim Jidi came back to him and, realizing he was approaching the end of life, he began to wonder what constituted being a real human and if he, indeed, were one. Sadly, he trudged back up to the mountain hut of Hakim Jidi. The sage greeted him as he had before.

"If you have traveled this far to see Hakim Jidi," he said,

"you must be in great need."

"I realize now," said Alab, "that I should have first become a real human before trying to create one out of clockwork."

So Alab remained with Hakim Jidi, until the ancient one returned to his ancestors, leaving Alab as his successor. So, if you are ever in great need, you can still ascend the mountain to ask help from the man who finally became real.

*This story was written in January 2025, a few weeks
after Trump began his second term as president. It
was inspired by two things: the contemporary political
situation most of all, but also by a true incident that
apparently happened to the father of a friend, Bob Israel.
As the story goes, Bob's father had created a healing
device that was impounded by some type of authories.*

The Medicus Animarum
of Dr. Israel

Following are transcripts of correspondence received concerning the device, reproduced in the order they were received by the Secretary of the International Science Symposium:

Written by Matthew Abbot:

November 10 ——————————————————————

For some reason, Hobbs kept coming in and out of my office this morning and I needed to look occupied. On a whim, I went to the Service's main site and searched for an inventory of the Secure Closet. I assumed there was no way we could function without one. Finally I found it.

It looks to me as if it gets updated weekly. Photos of each item, its filing number, and a brief case history. There's more stuff in there than I realized and no way to quickly locate an item based only on description. I just had to scroll through it. It took me hours, literally from about eleven a.m. to well into the afternoon. But at least I looked busy.

Things are always in the last place you look. I finally came across a square picture of the same color blue as the device. The photo looks to me as if it were taken from the bottom looking up. You can't see any wires or half-sphere, but I knew this had to be it. Strange, somebody would photograph it that way.

ISRAEL DEVICE. File #09106923054.

No case history. No date of seizure. No explanation of what it is. If I hadn't been curious before, I am now.

November 19

I think I might have made a terrible mistake. Right afterward, I thought about the saying, "curiosity killed the cat."

In the hallway this morning, I had run into Spencer, a guy I thought might know the building better than I did. I was right, he does. But I know very little about him. And these days, it pays to be suspicious until you have a good, solid reason to trust.

"Hey, Spencer. What's kept down in the basement?" I asked him in as casual a way as I could muster.

"The furnace, mostly," he said. "Why?"

"No special reason. I just wondered if we might have paper files stored down there. Stuff that's not been scanned."

That's when he looked at me in a way that made me instantly regret asking him. "Yeah," he said after a pause.

"There's shelves of bankers boxes with paper files stuffed in 'em. What's your interest?"

I tried to smile. "Oh, I have no special interest. Over at the Interior Department, they keep shit like that in the basement. I always thought it constituted a fire hazard."

His expression hadn't softened. "This is a concrete building, Abbot. If you're worried about it burning down, you're just looking for something to worry about." I turned to walk away. "There's no drugs down there, if that's what you're thinking," he called in a voice that everyone in the hallway heard. I decided to play his game.

"That's damn good," I said, looking back with the same expression he had. "Because if there were any, I promise you, Hobbs, heads would roll."

December 3 ——————————————————————————

I don't usually attribute random events to Fate. But I thought about it this morning when I spoke to Hobbs. I told him I had received a call from a company asking about the layout of the building—if there were a loading dock and a service elevator to the third floor.

He asked me what I had told the guy.

"Nothing," I said. "I wanted to check with you first."

"Get Spencer to call him back and give him whatever he wants. They're coming Friday to clear out everything in the Secure Closet."

The world began to wobble but I took a breath and said, "Oh. When you say cleared out, you mean...?"

"All that shit gets pulverized beyond recognition. They have clearance to dispose of our impounded material. They're the ones who burn weed for us. And, no, you can't watch. What's up with you, Abbot? You're the one who said the Closet was too full. I thought you'd be pleased."

"I am," I said, but I wasn't. I was panicked.

October 24

I'm sure the thing had been in the Secure Closet for at least weeks, if not months, before I noticed it. I had little reason to go into the Closet, which wasn't a closet at all but a dim room with no windows and a lock that would only open with my ID Card. The bulk of what was kept there looked like meth lab paraphernalia and counterfeiting presses. This thing was different. It was about 60 centimeters tall, wires draping over the sides and a half-spherical metal configuration that struck me somehow as elegant, if not downright artistic. Whoever manufactured it had taken a lot of trouble to encase it in molded blue plastic. It had been stashed in a corner with a piece of sheet metal covering most of it.

I only noticed it because the sheet metal was sharp and I was afraid that someone— maybe me—might run into it.

I had worked for the Department of the Interior for twelve years in Water Conservation. The new administration put a swift end to the entire Conservation Section, their goal being not to conserve water, but to maximize the profitability of polluting it. I guessed it was because I had spent two years in the National Guard that they didn't fire me like they did everyone else. I was transferred here to the US Marshalls Service where I'm painfully underemployed—making just a bit more than half my previous salary.

Susan, with whom I had planned our tenth anniversary, told me over and over to appreciate having a job at all. Everyone

I knew in government was either out of work or making less than I did. She's always had a knack keeping positive, unlike me. Hawaii got cancelled. I had no paid leave for another nine months. Her job was up for review so the school could keep its federal funding. I was hoping it would be in her favor that her husband worked for the Marshals Service and was therefore assumed to be one of the loyal guys.

I was so underemployed that I had to use strategies to keep looking busy. I started jotting down ideas in a small notebook that, of course, I kept on me at all times. It was out of pure boredom that I've started keeping a journal in it as well. God help me, I hope this isn't a fatal mistake.

November 26 ———————————————————————————

It's the day before Thanksgiving. There are so many people taking PTO that the entire building seems comfortably deserted. I purposely walked by Spencer's office this morning and saw his door was shut. At four o'clock, when even the most loyal workers were starting to leave, I took the stairs four flights down to the basement.

It's dark down there, stuffy and warm with the furnace blasting. It's much larger than I was expecting but, of course it is, because it runs the entire length of the building. I didn't even bother to look for a light switch. I had brought a head light.

Spenser is right. About ten meters from the furnace are long metal shelves, narrowly spaced. I had to be out of the building in an hour and the shelves seemed infinite. It was a hunch, really, that made me look for any section that might have been marked for Asset Recovery. According to guidelines, information on any confiscated property with an estimated value of over fifty grand would be there. And I had some idea from the file number that the seizure had happened sometime recently, maybe the past couple of months.

I felt driven—by what I didn't know, except I suspected that if the online inventory was sketchy, it had been done on purpose, especially if the property had been deemed highly valuable. I found an aisle cordoned off with police tape. I stepped over the ribbon. Red and black stickers over the boxes. At Interior that meant restricted. I have to admit my heart was pumping, and I started to worry that I should have worn gloves. I quickly got a hold of myself. No one was going to fingerprint a banker's box. I went through dozens of them, worrying instead about how much time I had left in that day. Folders weren't filed numerically by number, nor alphabetically by name of former property owner. I was about to give up. Then I pulled out this file:

ISRAEL, M. #09106923054. The folder had a seal over it. I broke it.

Most of the pages have been redacted. Why would anybody seal redacted files and put them in a restricted box? My headlamp was starting to dim. I ripped out a sheet from an adjoining file and started transcribing on the back.

Attorney General deems this property to
be extremely dangerous. Agents M4-17D,
M4-29, and M4-562 impounded the device from
the offices of Moishe Israel, Ph.D., of
[redacted] January 22, 2025 at 4:40 p.m.

Subject applied for U.S. Patent for the device,
listed on the application as Medicus Animarum.
Purpose stated on application: "Memory clarifier.
Consciousness enhancer." Subject had been
utilizing device in mental health practice,

The rest of the pages were redacted. A sealed envelope held several pages of schematics. I pocketed the envelope. Then my headlamp went out.

After I came home, I foolishly used my personal laptop to see if I could find anything on Moishe Israel, Ph.D. NOTE: Must be more careful in the future to use a public computer. Seems that all references to Moishe Israel and the Medicus Animarum have been removed from the Internet.

However, I came across this Reddit post:

r/newskid

An old guy up the street named Moishe stiffed me for a month's paper delivery. Found out he died yesterday. Can I sue anybody to get what he owes me?

The post was dated January 24, 2025. Two days after the raid on Moishe Israel's office.

November 17

The first email I received this morning was from Hobbs, asking me—telling me—to see him in his office at 10. I had no reason not be on time.

Hobbs is a large man, larger than is good for his health. If he ever finds this, I don't want him think I called him fat. But I would describe him as having been the kind of kid who struggled to keep up in school.

He was shuffling papers when I walked in. I figured they were my records.

"How do you like working at the Service, Abbot?" he asked without looking up.

"Great," I lied.

"Your boss at Interior said you were always a loyal employee."

"I try my best, sir."

"Good. Ever have any problems with drugs?"

"Nope."

"Ever tried them?"

"Nope," I lied again.

"Good. I see your wife is a teacher. What does she teach?

"Math," I aid, truthfully.

"I like math," he said, looking at me for the first time. "It's either right or it's wrong. Nothing vague or imaginary."

The idea of non-Euclidian geometry popped into my mind. "Not in middle school, sir."

He wrung his plump hands as if he were washing them. "Abbot, I see you've been in the Secure Closet three times this week."

"Yep," I said casually.

"How's come?"

I hadn't been expecting this. This was the first I was aware the system kept track of things like that, but I came up with something quick. "I don't know if you've been in there lately, but it's really crowded. I've been trying to move things around a little just in case we get new stuff to come in."

"You're not allowed to take anything out of there," he said.

"Article 9-115.2." I leaned forward just a little. People like Hobbs aren't hard to deal with. "I'll keep a sharp eye out, sir. If I ever suspect anything's out of order, I'll bring it to your attention immediately." He looked surprised. I winked. "You can count on me."

December 5 ————————————————————————————

The plan:

1.   Clock out for lunch but instead get wrench, screw drivers, hack saw, trash bag from Maintenance Room, 1st floor, rear.

2.   Go into Secure Closet and detach Israel device from plastic casing.

3.   Dismantle guts from one of the printing presses. Place inside casing.

4.   Place device in bag and put in my office trash can.

5.   Stay late, after hours, hide bag in basement in restricted area.

6.   While "clearing crew" has loading dock door open, take bag out through loading dock and lock in my trunk.

November 27 ————————————————————————————

We had dinner out on Wednesday and Susan's fam was over for Thanksgiving. It wasn't until we were in bed tonight that I read her my notes from the basement. It's now just after we talked, and I need to write down our conversation. For future refence:

"Are you saying you suspect the AG's Office of killing this guy?" she asked me, being level-headed as usual.

"Nothing says they killed anyone. I'm not saying it."

"But you're thinking it. What's happening to you, Matthew? You're turning into a conspiracy nut."

"What about the Reddit post? Two days after the raid."

"You think that would ever hold up in a court? It might not even be the same guy. Way too circumstantial. And, even if it were the same guy, maybe he got hit by a bus."

"Or killed himself?"

"We know those guys at the AG's Office are all nut cases. Mind-control machines? Please don't become one of them."

"But suppose there is something to it? A device that can help memory? Do you know how useful that would be in law enforcement? Enhance consciousness? God knows we need all the help we can get these days. Can you imagine if everyone in Congress was treated with a consciousness-raising machine?"

She laughed. "I would have liked to use it on the man who came to review us yesterday."

I turned on the electric blanket. "I forgot to ask. How did it go?"

She got quiet. It seemed as if it had been an innocent question. "Fine," was her quiet answer.

"No, it wasn't. I can tell."

"They asked me lots of questions about you."

"Me? What for?"

"I have no idea. How long you worked for the Department of Interior. Why did you leave? What did you do there? Had you ever coerced HR into hiring minorities?"

"What? That's not only racist, it's moronic."

"You know Andrea Cox, the librarian? She got fired. For some posters she had up."

"No!"

"I don't want to talk about it anymore. At least not now. I'll never get to sleep tonight."

We kissed and told each other we loved each other. I couldn't fall asleep. I kept wondering about Dr. Israel and what the Attorney General was so afraid of.

December 6 (morning) ———————————————————

As I suspected, the half-sphere is a helmet, but the wires are actually fiber optic cables. The whole thing uses zinc-air batteries like the kind used for hearing aids. Two of the cables are probably designed to be applied to the forehead by sensors with small suction cups, the other two to the back of the head. A glass tube like a longer version of a carpenter's level that seems intended to measure something. No controls, no instructions.

Susan is begging me not to experiment. She thinks that if the DOJ wanted the thing impounded it must be dangerous. She doesn't understand. There were projects I worked on at Interior that the new administration ordered, not just stopped, but erased completely. Projects I had spent years on, struggled with, poured every ounce of intelligence and experience into. Not to mention all my greatest hopes. It wasn't a matter of just believing in what we were doing, it was knowing how much it would benefit—not just farmers and the economy, but in saving lives. Why did they want to destroy and bury everything?

Was I angry? At myself for not doing at Interior what I had done at Marshall's Service? I felt as if I had sold my soul, and now not even able to make a decent living for my wife. No, I was furious. If I burn my brains out defying the Attorney General by using this machine, I don't care. Right after I get back from the store with batteries, I'll just see what happens.

 ————————————————————

At first it seemed like nothing at all. After fifteen minutes or so I was bored and disappointed. I worried that there might be an essential part of the device missing. My mind began to wander and, for no apparent reason, our wedding day came into my mind. But something felt slightly different. I was sitting at the head table at the reception, sipping the cheap champagne we had. I could recall the taste with unusual clarity and feel the pinch of my shoes. In the next moment I remembered walking the boardwalk at Ocean City with my friend Dave. I hadn't thought of that in decades, and yet I could clearly "see" the shirt he was wearing, "feel" the breeze, "smell" the ocean.

I got excited and tried to think about my first day of freshman year but nothing at all happened. I had no other sensations that I was aware of. No tingling. Nothing somatic. I relaxed and looked around the room, thinking that I should have drawn the curtains. Then I remembered being very young. Suddenly I recalled being a toddler in a playpen in the house where I grew up. I could see the color of the netting on the playpen and, through it, my mother talking on the phone. I knew she was talking to her friend Jane. They were discussing Jane's husband having an affair—something I could never had understood at the time. But my excitement caused it to dissolve.

For an hour I stayed hooked to the device. Susan came in periodically to check on me. I kept telling her I was fine. As far as I could tell, I was. I did ask her if she knew what happened to the denim skirt with the mustard stain that she was wearing when we first met on the day when cirrus clouds were over the Italian Ice stand. She just shook her head and walked out.

There seemed to be no organization to the memories that the device provoked. They came randomly and well out of chronological order. What they all had in common was the vividness of the recall—something approximating a dream, yet I felt fully conscious. The more I tried, the less happened, and I wondered if Israel used hypnosis in conjunction with the device. I tried not to think at all or, rather, since that is impossible, I just let my mind wander. That's when the memories would appear.

I began to take notes, but realized that meant trying too hard. Eventually, probably due staying relaxed, I noticed that a silver vapor appeared in the glass tube every time I had a memory. And, the most fascinating part of it was that it seemed the further to the right the vapor reached, the more recent the memory. A memory of my interview with the Marshalls Office was far to the right. A memory of grade school was to the left.

If there were any danger in the device, I decided, it was that it was becoming too much fun. My moments back in time were tantalizingly brief and frustratingly random. Israel probably never intended for his patients to sit for hours re-living moments from their past. There had to be a more directed purpose. But what?

Just as I was about to decide to switch it off, something entirely unexpected happened. I remembered being in total darkness with no bodily sensations other than a feeling I was moving forward. In fact, I felt as if I had no body at all. Then there was a light ahead of me, first dim, then growing as I "approached" it. There were people in this light—people I knew that I knew but couldn't recognize. Something extremely significant was happening. Was I remembering my own birth?

The thought was incredibly intriguing, and my emotions caused the memory to dissolve.

I looked at the glass tube. I expected to see the silver vapor all the way to the left, but it wasn't. I was all the way to the right. Past the mark on the glass.

Was I remembering the future?

Written by Susan Abbot:

To: Secretary of the International Science Symposium
Spui 70. 2511 BT, Den Haag, Netherlands

March 30

It's been nearly four months since my husband died of injuries inflicted by the thugs who broke into our house with no warning or warrant and destroyed the Medicus Animarum. I thought I would be paralyzed by grief forever—but I had been given some help.

Last month when I started going through the house in order to put it on the market, I was preoccupied, as always, with what happened. Somehow—and I'm convinced this is far more than coincidence—I began to wonder what my husband was thinking in the day before the tragedy. I had a hunch to look in our bedroom closet, although it had been thoroughly ransacked. I pulled out the shoe box we called "The Memory Chest."

It's full of random, useless things like photos of us as kids, ticket stubs, the itinerary for the trip to Hawaii. But underneath a false bottom I found his journal, along with an envelope containing schematic drawings for the Animarum. The last page of Matthew's journal had a note addressed to me. It was the name and address of someone he had met while working for Interior. It was you and your address abroad.

I cut up Matthew's journal and mailed it in random pieces to your address. I mailed it from as many different post offices as I could go to without raising suspicion. In case any of the letters were intercepted, I didn't want any one of them to tell the entire story.

I told my school I need to visit my cousin in New York City. Once I'm safely outside the country, we can post scans of the device on the Internet and mail copies to every university outside the U.S. that might have an interest. In the meantime, I will put this note into an envelope with international postage and mail to my cousin to forward to you.

The help I had in getting through the impossible last few months came from something I had kept secret. In the middle of the night before the raid, I tried the Animarum on myself. Like Matthew, I witnessed lots of vivid images from my childhood. Then something unexplainable happened. I "remembered" images of the raid that hadn't yet happened, the funeral and, finally, myself, the guest at an international award for scientific achievement. I have no explanation. I'm writing this with no speculation or comment.

I look forward to meeting you when I arrive in town.

BTW: I looked up an English meaning of the Latin name of the device. It translates to something like *Healer of Souls*.

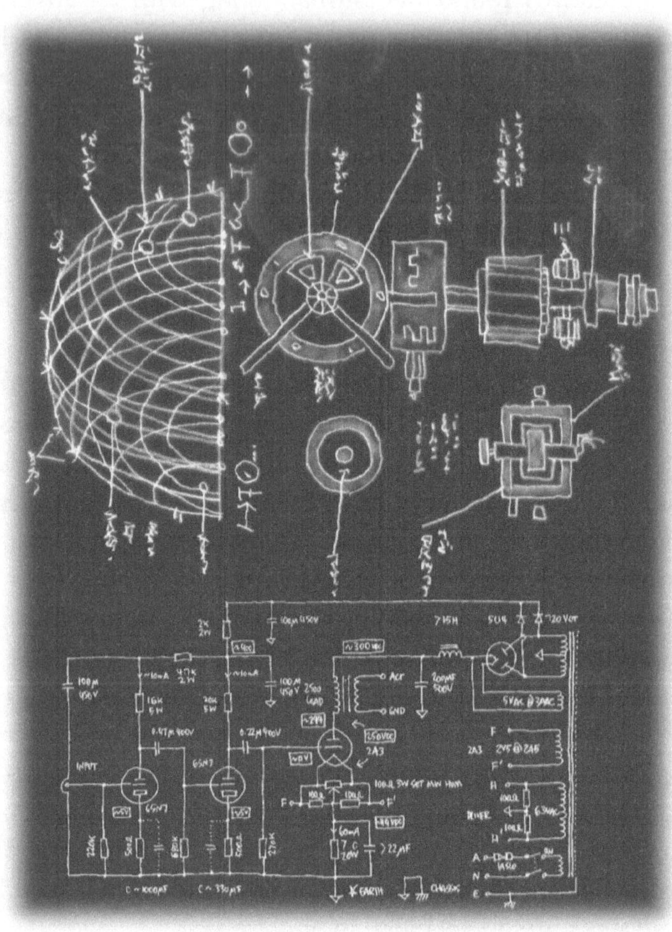

186

The Soul of Pietro

Once in a distant land, a certain man's fortune required him to undertake a sea voyage on a vital mission. During the journey, a sudden storm wrecked the ship, killing everyone except this one man. He was knocked nearly unconscious but managed to cling to a piece of wood and eventually was washed ashore on a forlorn island.

He was finally discovered clinging to a rock by some fishermen who lived nearby. These people and their families were the only inhabitants of this remote place. They brought the man into their cluster of meager huts and, after nursing him back to health, gave him a shelter of his own.

The man had been badly hurt in the catastrophe, and his ability to speak was impaired, although he was, in any event, ignorant of the language of the local people. What was even more challenging was that he had lost all memory of his life before the shipwreck. Because he couldn't remember even his own name, the villagers called him Pietro.

The fishermen eventually taught Pietro how to catch fish so he would be able to survive. But, because of Pietro's injuries, it was difficult for him to become as efficient as they were. Besides, Pietro was a person of small stature, unlike the other village men who had developed great strength from years of rowing their boats through the turbulent waves. Eventually, though, Pietro managed to catch enough fish to keep himself alive.

Of course, the life Pietro led was a lonely one. Because of his speech accent and unfamiliarity with the local language, it was difficult for him to communicate with anyone. The unmarried women in the village had little interest in him, as they judged men on their ability to catch fish, and Pietro could barely feed himself. Even more painful, Pietro had no memories to sustain and support him in the hours spent alone fishing in his little boat or lying in the threadbare hammock in his hut.

After a great many years in which life went on uneventfully for Pietro, a small boat appeared on the horizon. It came to land on the beach in front of the village and an old man in a patched cloak came ashore. Although he was unable to speak their language, the stranger greeted the locals with small gifts such as sewing needles, fruit, and hardtack.

At first excited by the prospect of the new arrival, Pietro soon became disappointed when he realized that the stranger wasn't able to understand his speech any more than the villagers. That evening, the entire community held a gathering around a great fire on the beach to celebrate the visitor's arrival.

The stranger remained in the village for two days. While he replenished his supply of fresh water, it seemed to Pietro, he was also studying the people and their lives. The visitor tried to demonstrate to the fishermen how they could attach rudders to the underside of their primitive rowboats to stabilize their crafts. The locals listened to the instruction with polite tolerance but without much understanding.

When the visitor began to prepare to leave the island, Pietro asked to join him, but the old man showed him that his boat was capable of holding only one. As he was about to leave, the stranger looked at Pietro for what seemed a long time. He disappeared into the hold of his tiny craft, brought out something wrapped in a cloth, and gave it to Pietro before leaving the island forever.

Back in his hut, Pietro unwrapped the parcel, discovering a chisel and a hammer. He could make nothing of the gift's purpose at first, but, as the days went on, he began to feel it must hold some significance. He wondered if the tools were meant to be symbolic, but of what, he couldn't guess.

When he was able to find the time, Pietro built a rudder for his own boat, and the addition did, in fact, help the stability of the vessel. Some of the other fishermen were amused, others taunted him, but they all seemed to be unwilling to try to change the way they, as had generations before them, navigated in the water. Besides, none held a great deal of respect for Pietro, as he was the least successful among them and spoke hesitantly and, at best, with an impediment.

One day not long after the stranger left, while Pietro was fishing, his line became tangled with a small piece of driftwood. After cursing his own luck, but before he could toss the wood back into the waves, he noticed that the object had the rough shape of a fish. Taking the driftwood back to his hut that evening, Pietro took the chisel and, in the low light of evening, cut at the wood until it very much resembled a fish, complete with fins, scales, eyes, and a mouth.

He scoured the shore the next day and collected bits of wood that had previously only seemed like hazards. Day after day, when his work was done, Pietro carved objects from what he had collected. He carved the shapes of fish of different kinds, jewelry, and even bowls and utensils. When he had a collection of these artifacts, he thought of the stranger's offerings to the villagers, and distributed his carvings as gifts to all.

Unfamiliar with crafts, the local people were at first suspicious, but they agreed that because of Pietro's many limitations, what he was doing would not pose a threat. For his part, Pietro felt he was repaying the villagers for saving his life.

One night, months later, a terrible storm blew across the island. The sounds and the wind terrified Pietro and stirred up his memories of having been once nearly killed in a shipwreck. He tried for hours to keep the terrible memories from tormenting him and finally fell into a restless sleep. In what was more delirium than dream, Pietro had a vision of an angelic being coming to comfort him in his desperation. When he woke, he was haunted by the dream and the vividness of the vision.

In the calm of the next morning, Pietro found that the trunk of a large tree had washed on the beach near his hut. When some of the fishermen began to drag it out of the way, Pietro asked them to help him haul it to a small rise behind his hut. As he stood looking at the huge piece of wood, he began to imagine the form of the being of his dream. The more he stared, the more he was able to visualize the celestial being, as if she were somehow imprisoned in the substance of the tree trunk.

Rather than spend the day fishing, Pietro took his hammer and chisel and began to carve into the wood. Day after day he persisted and slowly the form of a figure, draped in soft folds of a garment, reaching its hands to offer comfort, emerged from the rough, storm-tossed shape of the wood.

As he worked, something emerged in him as well.

Although he still wasn't able to remember his life before the accident, he became more and more aware that he was not actually Pietro. He knew he was someone else, someone who belonged to a different world, with a different purpose than the basic survival needed for life on the island. By the time the sculpture was completed to his own satisfaction, he realized that he no longer cared what the local people thought of him, or if they thought of him at all. He still lived alone, of course, but his loneliness gradually left him.

In the years that followed, he continued to sculpt wood which washed on the beach or fell in the forest behind the village. He gave trinkets freely to anyone who would accept. On the sandy ridge, he created many statues that, over the years, gradually fell victim to wind and rain.

When this man took his final breath, he was taken up in the arms of his ancestors, truly knowing who he really was.

Other Books by Jonathan D. Scott

Lenegrin

The Woman in the Wilderness

Gunther's Revenge (as Guy Bandervilt)

Yasmine and the Million Dollar Jacket (as Terry Baldwin)

Tess, Terrorists. and the Tiara (as Terry Baldwin)

Warren Pieces